Triple Crown Publications
Presents

Diva

By
KANE & ABEL

This is a work of fiction. The authors have invented the characters. Any resemblance to actual persons, living or dead, is purely coincidental.

Compilation and Introduction copyright © 2004 by
Triple Crown Publications
2959 Stelzer Road Suite C
Columbus, Ohio 43219
www.TripleCrownPublications.com

Library of Congress Control Number: 2004102062
ISBN# 0-9747895-8-5
Cover Design/Graphics: www.MarionDesigns.com
Editor: Kathleen Jackson
Consulting: Vickie M. Stringer

First Trade Paperback Edition Printing April 2004

Printed in the United States of America

Dedications

This book is dedicated to the 1,000,000 loyal fans that purchased our records. Also, to the fallen soldiers that we lost to the streets.

In loving memory: Anthony Rodriguez, Urbano Rodriguez, Edward "Big Ed" Knight, Luis "Matrix" Conerly, Clarence Landry, Big Otis, Gerardo and Concepcion Garcia, Joseph Henry, and Monty.

Acknowledgements

This book is dedicated to the Garcia, Rodriguez, and Rosario families. Special thanks to Mrs. Maumus, Ms. Connelly, Mrs. Anatole. Shout out to Xavier University, Big Doc, E, Los, Craigo, Mom, Delano, Madi, Shaun, Tony, Rich, Ray, Edward, Ruben, Chrissie, Sarah, Sylvana, George, Jojo, Jessica, Anthony, Lil George, Tito, Monica, Nat, Marlene, Candice, Grandpa, Grandma, Free, Wild Wayne, Angela, Lil D, Meedy, Adrian, Marceilla and fam, Tony El Malo, Snoop, Lil Jon, Lil Scrappy, Ulysses, Shannon Holmes, Vickie Stringer, Da Brat, Juvenile, Aubrey, BG, Young City, Roy Jones Jr., Choppa, Boss Hog, Mel, Weebie, Manni Fresh, Kenny, Funk Master Flex, Mimi Valdes, Betsy Bolte, Ice Blue Harris at the Source, Ocean Macadams, Jim Colson, Bobby Bland, Tracey Edmonds,

Julian and Jeneba at Edmonds Ent., Delano, BlackIyce, Street Ballers, Lil Wayne, Soupa, Trick Daddy, T.I., The Diplomats and Cam, Marco, Tia, Big Dave, Doodah, Dene, Mimi, Doogie, Fat Mama, JK, Ruff Ryders, DMX, Big Tigga, Big Daddy Kane, Special Ed, DJ Kool, Rosta Man, Crazy and fam, Sarah T. Reed, Tap, E, Supa Mike, Tweezy, PJ, Box, Royale, Dolby D, Troy D, Mojo, Chill, Keith, Chip, Luther Speight, Blunt Wraps, Mia X, No Limit, David Banner, Lil Flip, Papa Rue, One Dub, Porter, Dre, Lundy, Young Dirty, and All of our fam on lock down.

Rest In Peace

Anthony Rodriguez, Edward "Big Ed" Knight, Urbano Rodriguez, Louis "Matrix" Conerly, Gerardo and Concepcion Garcia, Clarence Landry, Big Otis, Curl, Joseph Henry, Biggie Smalls, Tupac, LeftEye, Terrence "Lil daddy" Mckenzie.

Chapter 1

Jenny stood in the spacious living room, peering out of the curtain. She knew Delilah would be there any minute because she hated to be late. Jenny checked her surroundings once more to make sure everything was set. Detail after detail spun through her mind, until she was satisfied that she had not forgotten anything. Everything had to be just right, because she knew the time had come to make her move. She checked and rechecked her steps.

Jenny was a perfectionist, which was one of the reasons she was Delilah's personal assistant. Despite them being friends for so long, Jenny's organizational skills were immaculate, which made Delilah rely on her more and more. Jenny was more than competent enough to manage her friend's blossoming career.

She controlled Delilah's finances, making sound investments with her money. She protected her friend from all the negative trappings of fame and wealth. She watched out for the unscrupulous accountants, with their can't miss stock tips, and so-called sound investments choices. When one possessed money, the con artists would crawl out of the woodworks, with the get rich quick schemes, not to mention the star struck groupies and stalkers. Delilah definitely had her share of those. They were fans that were absolutely obsessed with Delilah, almost worshipping her as if she were a Goddess. Forming a protective wall around her friend, Jenny put together a team of top-notch security guards, attorneys and accountants, which she often referred to as "Team Delilah", and on this team, she was the coach.

Everyday she laid down the game plan and executed it to perfection.

Jenny made it possible for Delilah to concentrate on her singing. Her girl had her back and not some stranger she had hired. For all her hard work, Jenny was compensated and, she drew a six-figure check from Delilah annually. Other than her grandmother, Jenny was the only person in the world that Delilah trusted. Besides placing her career in her hands, Delilah would trust Jenny with her life, if necessary.

Of course, Jenny would have loved to be in the spotlight too. She remembered the days when she, Sasha and Delilah were young fourth graders in pigtails and jelly shoes, when they first thought about being a singing group. They had dreams of being bigger stars than TLC and EnVogue put together. Just the thought of those memories made Jenny giggle. But once Delilah met KB and he introduced them to

Big Rock, Delilah had no choice but to go solo, or so she said.

"Well fuck them!" Jenny remembered Sasha exclaim. "We don't need no Big Rock!"

"Sasha, girl this is a once in a lifetime opportunity for us." Delilah tried to convince her.

"For us? No, for you! How you gonna even play us like that Dee. I thought we was 'posed to be girls?" Sasha retorted.

Jenny knew Sasha was still upset about KB picking Delilah over her. Now, the solo deal was like the straw that broke the camel's back.

"You hear this shit, Jenny?" Sasha asked, but Jenny never once voiced the deep disappointment she felt in her heart.

Jenny was a pretty girl, but it was clear who the star was, it wasn't hard to see why they picked Delilah. Both Jenny and Delilah were strikingly pretty, but Jenny's light hazel brown eyes and chiseled facial features almost looked strange. Jenny was a short and extremely frail looking Puerto Rican. Her naturally dark brown hair was bleached, streaked and highlighted to a golden blonde color. Guys would often tell her that she was pretty, but she didn't believe them, thinking it was all a game to get into her drawers. Her good looks did nothing for her self-esteem, actually it worked against her, making her overly self-conscious.

Delilah, on the other hand, was a tall, curvaceous, light skinned black girl with long curly hair that reached the center of her back. Her voice was unmistakable. Delilah could hit high notes like no one else. She had the God given ability to sing any popular song and make it her own. This wonderful combination made her a force to be reckoned with in the music industry and Jenny knew she'd take the entertainment world by storm. Sasha must have been a fool not to, at least, attach herself to Delilah's imminent success.

"Yo, I'm outta here. I don't play second fiddle to no bitch." Sasha told Delilah, then turned to Jenny and added. "You comin', J?"

Jenny looked from Sasha to Delilah and back again. She too felt betrayed by Delilah but she loved Delilah too much to just walk away.

"Well?" Sasha impatiently reiterated.

Jenny just dropped her head. She didn't have the self-respecting pride to leave, or the spine to stay.

"Then, fuck you too!" Sasha spat, as she slammed the door behind her. She hadn't spoken to them since.

It had taken sometime, but Jenny finally realized her position in life and she played it well. However, she always secretly hoped that one day she'd be the center of attention. She prayed that that day had finally arrived.

The blowing of the horn let her know Delilah was there. She peeked out of the window once more and saw the stretch Hummer limo waiting at the curb. It was a cool,

6

overcast day in New York City, but excitement filled the air.

Jenny threw on her coat and grabbed her bags on the way out

the door.

The driver stepped out and opened the door for

Delilah. When she saw Delilah exit the limo, Jenny couldn't

contain her happiness. She was so glad to see her girl. As

Jenny started to run up to the car, Delilah ran towards her,

and they wrapped each other in a loving hug in the middle of

the block. The driver began to place Jenny's multitude of

suitcases into the trunk.

"Hey girl!" Jenny screeched. "What's really good?"

"Same ole shit, ma!" Delilah smiled.

"I haven't seen you in a hot minute! What is the deal?

How is grandma?"

Delilah released Jenny from the bear hug and settled

for an arm around the shoulder.

"She's aiight. Buggin' out as usual. She won't even

let me move her out of the hood, into a co-op or condo.

Somewhere safe, anywhere but there. God forgive me for sayin' this, but that building is gonna be the death of her. Shit is getting worse round there, not better. I worry 'bout my grandmother when I'm out on tour. I mean, what's the sense of havin' money if you can't take care of the hands that took care of you, huh? She is battlin' Alzheimer disease and still hardheaded and stubborn as ever, but other than that, she's good though."

Jenny rubbed her friend's hand lovingly. "It'll be fine, ma. Hold ya head up and pray, that's all. You got control over nobody but yourself. Some people never change and ya grandmom happens to be one of them people. Don't even stress it, let her be. God willing, she'll be fine. She's a soldier. She made it all these years by herself. Anyway, did you send old girl my love? Did you tell her I miss her?"

"You know I did. She said to tell her sumthin' she don't know, and you better come see about her soon too. You ain't too big for her to whup ya ass either. My grandma's a real trip, she still thinks she can take on the world and win. She don't even realize that we've gotten bigger and she don't scare us no more." Delilah said, laughiing.

Continuing to make idle talk, the two friends walked quickly back to the Hummer. Steadfast, the driver stood by impatiently holding the door oopen. Once the two occupants were safely inside, he shut the door and quickly raced around to the driver's side.

"Well." Jenny said. "You know we got WZKZ in L.A. at nine tonight, The Late Show after that and then Intersound has a triple platinum party for you starting at midnight."

"Wow." Delilah sighed. "They doin it up big, it's like that?"

"Yeah girl, it's like that. You deserve everything they doin'. Have you seen the numbers you been doin' lately? You had the number one album in the country for twelve weeks straight. Right now, you that bitch! Ain't nobody fuckin' wit you."

Delilah giggled at her friend's comment.

"You better get all the private time on the plane, cause when we land, it's on and poppin'. We gotta hit the ground runnin'. When you're on top, everybody wants a piece of you. As they say, gotta pay the cost to be the boss! That's what happens when you've got the top selling album in the country!"

Delilah smirked, while pulling out her cell phone.

Jenny's eyebrows suddenly raised high out of curiosity. "Gimme that, girl! You kick back and relax, I'll check all your messages and answer the most important ones. Now get some rest ma, you gotta look extra pretty tonight. Don't ask why either, I'll tell you later."

Delilah kicked back and rested her eyes. It would be at least thirty minutes until they got to the airport. She figured she'd just call and check in with her grandma when they got there. She wanted to keep her aware of her movements.

Intently, Jenny listened to each voice message left on Delilah's phone.

"Delilah, this is Rick Jonathan. I've been trying to get in touch with you, it's real important we talk. I have the information you asked about. Call me."

"This is Bernard Johnson from Tri-Max Films. Please call me as soon as your schedule permits. We're really excited about working with you. Have your attorney call the office."

"Yo, Delilah this is your man Big Rock. Word up ma, I miss you and I'm sorry about all this other shit, for real. Holla at me as soon as you can. I love you. One!"

Jenny sucked her teeth at the sound of Big Rock's voice.

"What?" Delilah asked. Lately, every time Big Rock's name came up or he was around, Jenny started acting funny.

"Nothin." Jenny replied, still checking messages.

"Then what was," Delilah mimicked Jenny's teething sucking, "all about?"

Jenny replied. "I don't know, I just think you could do better, you know? He act like it's all about you behind closed doors, but then he act all fly when we out and about. I just don't be feelin' the way he treats you.

Delilah just looked at her friend lovingly. Jenny hadn't changed since high school, she still had Delilah's back to the fullest. Anybody else would've been overwhelmed that the number one rapper was feeling her best friend, but Delilah felt that Jenny really cared. Still, there was something deeper that Delilah couldn't put her finger on. Even though her life seemed to be all bling, bling and champagne, behind the façade, things were going too fast. Her life wasn't her own anymore and all of the issues that have been occurring lately had her head in a spin. She needed a vacation, a get-away from all the madness and the spotlight. Delilah told herself she'd fly down to the Virgin Islands as soon as her schedule would allow. She needed to recharge her batteries, relax and enjoy the little things in life. But first, she needed to deal with all the issues at hand.

"Jen." Delilah said.

"Yeah Dee, what's up?" Jenny asked innocently.

"When we get to L.A., let's talk, like we used to back in the day. I really need to holla at you cause I got a lot on my mind and I need to get if off my chest."

Jenny smiled. " No doubt. Whenever you're ready, I'm all ears."

Delilah was glad she had that attitude, but she wasn't so sure Jenny would feel the same way after they talked. Exhausted, Delilah laid her head back and stretched out in the spaciousness of the Hummer. She valued sleep, because in that state she was free from all the stress that had been wearing heavily on her lately.

Jenny looked at her friend, and again for the thousandth time, wondered how it would feel to be her. She knew about the stress factor involved with fame and fortune, but the accolades were something she wanted to experience. Jenny felt Delilah's life was like a movie, and she patted herself on the back for being such a good director. Jenny needed Delilah, but Jenny knew Delilah needed her as well and it felt good to be appreciated.

Delilah began to drift into dreamland as the Hummer bounced along to their destination. Tomorrow this'll be all over, Delilah's mind sang. Tomorrow, I'll be able to, that was her last thought before her tranquility was shattered like the window behind her head, followed by an ear piercing scream and the sound of screeching tires.

There would be no tomorrow for Delilah Brown, no Caribbean get away, no more songs would she sing, but there

14

would also be no more stress, as the Hummer began to flip end over end.

A sharp pain suddenly shot through Melinda Brown's right hand causing, her to drop the needle and thread she was holding. She began to gently message her aching joints with the opposite hand. She grimaced in pain as she glanced up at the cuckoo clock mounted on her bedroom wall. She suddenly realized that the hours had quickly passed. She was certain that Delilah had made her flight and landed safely in Los Angeles by now. Repeatedly, she tried calling her cell phone, but got no response, as her calls continued to go straight to Delilah's voicemail. This fact disturbed Melinda a great deal. This wasn't like her granddaughter at all. She was always a nervous wreck whenever her granddaughter had to fly. Melinda didn't trust airplanes one bit, not with all the crashes that were happening today. The more she tried to get it out of her mind, the more she thought about it. "Lord, please let my grandbaby be safe and sound." She silently prayed. The old woman tried to get out of the worrying habit that she had developed, but it was hard. Once you pass a certain age, you inadvertently get set in your ways.

To her, there was nothing more important in the world than her grandchild. She loved her to death. Delilah was the centerpiece of her life, she couldn't bear to even think about losing her baby. She had already lost her own daughter, Felicia. She hoped and prayed Delilah was just too busy to call. If so, it would be a once in a lifetime oversight on her part. After all, she is human, and humans make mistakes. "Yeah, maybe she's tied up doing a TV or radio interview or something." She thought to herself, she'll call soon, I know it. Doesn't she always? Maybe she was just taking care of business first.

In the past, Delilah had always checked in with her grandmother. A simple five-minute call went a long way in calming her already shaky nerves. Though Melinda refused to believe the funny feeling that lay deep in her gut, she knew something was seriously wrong. Her maternal instinct told her so. The fact that her granddaughter hadn't called yet was surprising, normally she would have called by now. "What was going on?" She questioned. "Maybe I'm just overreacting." She thought, as she grabbed the remote control and flipped on the TV. "Let me stop fussing over that child she ain't no baby. She grown now."

Around this time of day, she usually watched the daily news. Right now, she wasn't in the mood for the horror stories the news had in store for its viewers. She had her own problems, she didn't need to hear about anyone else's. So, instead, she tuned into one of those cheesy talk shows about rebellious teens or broken relationships. She desperately wanted to lighten the glum mood that had engulfed her. Melinda got a real kick out of how ignorant some people could actually behave, especially in front of a live and national audiences of maybe millions. To her, it was amusing and sad at the same time, the dumb stuff that came flying out their mouths. She thought the only thing all those people needed was a good old-fashioned ass whooping. That would learn them a good lesson, she mused.

Suddenly her show was interrupted by a special news bulletin. She tried to change the channel, hoping it was only on that station. She found the exact same thing on every station she turned to. Finally, she gave in and paid full attention to the news bulletin. She winced her eyes tightly, trying to focus on the screen. Still, it was a struggle for her to see the screen clearly from that distance.

The solemn faced anchorman began. "We interrupt your regularly scheduled program to bring you this late breaking news."

Mesmerized, Melinda sat glued to the television screen, hanging onto every word the reporter said. She turned up the volume button and listened intently, she didn't want to miss a thing. She knew whatever the announcement, it had to be a major crisis or something to cut into the show's airtime. Maybe it was a weather advisory or some presidential state of the union address.

Continuing, the anchorman spoke very slowly. It gave his announcement a greater impact. "This afternoon, while traveling to the airport, singer Delilah Brown, multi-platinum superstar R&B crooner, was involved in a terrible car accident. Reports are sketchy at the moment. We'll update you more as additional information is made available. However, there are believed to be no survivors."

Melinda saw a picture of the crushed stretch Hummer on the highway. It was flipped over and fumes were in the air. There were fire trucks, police and emergency workers running in every direction like swarming bumblebees to honey.

"In case you are just tuning in, yes, it has just been confirmed, music superstar, Delilah Brown and her assistant, Jenny Santiago, have been killed in a fatal car crash. The cause of the accident is unknown at this time. Once again,

Delilah Brown and her assistant, Jenny Santiago, are both confirmed dead." Suddenly, the anchor pressed his right hand against a slightly visible earpiece. Then he quickly relayed the message he had just received. "I've just received word that the limousine driver, whose name was Rodney Simmons, has also been confirmed dead. I repeat, Rodney Simmons, the driver, has also been confirmed dead."

Numb with pain, Melinda felt as if someone had just squeezed the little bit of life she had remaining out of her body. The anchorman might as well have been speaking Chinese, because from that point on, she couldn't understand a word he was saying. There must be some mistake, she reasoned. Refusing to believe what she had just heard, her head began to feel heavy. She was in a daze. Her knees wobbled uncontrollably. She felt a tremendous pressure on her chest as she collapsed to the floor. Tears fought to escape her old eyes, but there was something holding them back. A scream from deep inside of her struggled to leave her mouth, but the sound never left her throat. This couldn't be real.

"Lord, Jesus please! This can't be. No dear God! It can't be. How could you do this to me? Not again! This is too much pain for one lifetime. This has to be a bad dream, a nightmare. It just has to be." She prayed aloud.

Due to the fatal news she had received, Melinda began to tremble violently on the bed. She silently wished that the Lord would just take her now. She couldn't imagine living one more day without her grandchild. Finally, the screams made their way out of her desperate lungs. "Please God! Please let it be a nightmare!" She yelled, and then she fell unconscious.

Chapter 2

As Detectives Nilo and Scott drove toward the crime scene, the DJ on the radio gave Delilah his eulogy. "Superstar, Diva and R&B angel, Delilah Brown, will truly be missed. We love you Delilah and we'll forever mourn you. It was a pleasure to have you grace this earth with your immense talent and wonderful presence. May you rest in peace."

The words summed up Detective Elijah Scott's sentiments exactly. Scott to loved Delilah Brown because she was from the old neighborhood, which was his own neighborhood. It felt good to have the Bronx known for more than just drugs and violence. He was proud of her accomplishments. Det. Scott had even met Delilah a few times, and each time, he cherished those moments. She seemed to be so sweet and humble, so down to earth. He had personally asked to be assigned to the case because he felt so emotionally involved. He knew it would be a tough case, but one he had no choice but to commit to.

He didn't, however, ask for his current partner, Detective Tony Nilo, a hard-nosed middle aged Italian from Bensonhurst. Det. Nilo was a ballbuster, and Scott suspected, a closet racist. But overall, Det. Nilo was a good cop and the Captain personally assigned him to the case as well. They wanted this case cleared up, and fast, because the whole city loved Delilah Brown. They had lost one of their own. She was such a talented young woman who had a clean, wholesome image. There were no controversies swirling around her, or no gossip had ever been uttered in the same sentence as her name. She had done so much good for the community, giving back as a role model and volunteer. Just a few weeks ago, she was presented with an honorary key to the city.

When they arrived, forensic investigators crowded the scene of the crime. With a fine-tooth comb, they searched for any little piece of evidence. They knew the tiniest clue could break the case wide open. There were long yellow police ribbons on all sides, blocking the site from public entry. Traffic was backed up on both sides of the Van Wyck expressway for miles. Commuters, straining their necks to see, made it equally as hard to drive on either side. Horns were blowing angrily. Noisy news helicopters hovered from overhead, trying to get a good aerial view for their respective newscasts. Reporters seemed to be everywhere, even in restricted, taped off areas that they didn't have access to, but this was headline news. Any scoop that they could get might possibly boost their career. It could take any reporter from field correspondent to lead anchor. Delilah's tragic death created a media frenzy, taking on a circus like atmosphere. She was so adored by the public. Young girls cried solemnly as they passed the collision site, as if they personally witnessed the fatal accident.

A huge public outcry erupted over the way Delilah's remains were handled. Somehow a news helicopter was able to get a close up of her scarred body. It was a gruesome sight for even the hardest of hearts. This added fuel to the fire, Delilah's death was quickly becoming a public spectacle, one that had no end in sight.

"If you take one more of them pictures, I'm takin your fuckin camera!" Det. Nilo barked at an over anxious reporter, as he and Det. Scott pushed through the thickened crowd. The cool morning air circulated the smoke from the accident. The crash was so violent it looked like a missile had hit the vehicle. Nilo lit up a cigarette, taking in the scenery. He glanced over at Scott, who appeared to be lost in his own thoughts.

"I take it, this one hit close to home, huh?" Det. Nilo asked Det. Scott. He was aware of the fact that Scott had asked for the case.

Det. Scott looked at him and replied. "I guess you could say that. It's just too tragic to think about. She was so beautiful."

Not anymore, Det. Nilo thought to himself, while looking at her charred remains. "You gonna be alright?" Nilo asked.

"I have to be." Scott replied.

Det. Nilo thumped his cigarette to the ground. "Forensics says each victim had gunshot wounds to the head. This one looks like it could get messy." Nilo commented, and Scott merely nodded then sighed. "Then I guess we haven't anytime to lose."

"Any idea where to start?" Nilo asked.

"I think we should go by and see her grandmother." Scott answered, then headed back towards the car.

As he watched the news, Big Rock couldn't believe his ears. Dead? Delilah, dead? The two words wouldn't agree in his mind. How? Why? The vivid image of the mangled Hummer played over and over in his mind. So many answerless questions filled his thoughts and a sixth sense told him to get out of the hotel room he was in. He got up, blew out the candles, grabbed the unopened bottle of Armadele and his coat, and then quickly shot out the door.

It was nothing more than an ordinary day at the Federal Correctional Institution in Texarkana, Texas. Somehow, unforeseen trouble was brewing in the air.

"Ay yo KB! KB, come here quick!"

KB was lying on his bed reading the book, "B More Careful" when he heard his man Scooby's voice, sounding urgent. He quickly laced up his sneakers and ran out his cell to the day room to see what was so urgent. When he got there, you could hear a pin drop as the other inmates turned

from the TV to steal glances of his awaited reaction.

"Yo son, its Delilah, she dead, yo." Scooby

sorrowfully informed him.

KB just looked at his man for any sign of a joke, but

he knew Scooby didn't play like that. He directed his

attention to the screen just in time to hear Free on 106 and

Park say. "We're all gonna miss Delilah Brown. It seems

like yesterday when she first came in here to promote her

first CD." Free's voice failed off in tears as AJ tried to

console her.

"She was in an accident, player. Dead on the scene.

Police are investigating the accident."

But KB knew it was no accident. He knew exactly

what happened and he knew what he needed to do. Without

hesitation, he headed back to his cell and began to fire off a

letter to his man Pinky Blades, written in Harlem code

words. Then he wrote to his baby mama, Sasha. He smiled to himself just thinking of the job he had for her to do.

Dets. Nilo and Scott arrived in front of Melinda Brown's building and went inside. The way Scott moved, Nilo felt Scott had been there before, a fact he filed away in his sharp detective mind. When they arrived on the 6th floor, they knocked politely on Ms. Brown's door. After a few minutes had passed, there was still no answer. Det. Scott tried the doorknob, and it was open. They both eased their pistols out of their holsters and walked in.

"Ms. Brown?" Det. Scott called out and waited for a reply.

No response.

"Ms. Brown, this is the NYPD, are you in there?"

Still there was no response. The two detectives ventured in cautiously. They both spotted Ms. Brown sprawled out on the floor and rushed to her side. Nilo checked her pulse.

"She's alive." Nilo informed Scott with a sigh of relief, and then firmly shook her shoulders.

After the second shake, she finally began to stir. As her eyes slowly opened, they revealed two large blurry objects coming into focus. The strange faces glaring down on her made Ms. Brown tense up instinctively.

"Who are you?" She managed to ask.

"Relax ma'am, let me help you up." Det. Nilo offered, but Ms. Brown snatched away.

"Not until you tell me who you are and what you're doing in my apartment." She said.

The old woman may have looked sickly, but Det. Nilo could tell she still had her wits about her. He flashed his badge and said. "Detective Tony Nilo of NYPD and this is Detective Elijah Scott. Please allow me to help you to the couch."

Ms. Brown relented and Det. Nilo helped her to the couch, while Det. Scott went into the kitchen and got her a glass of water.

"I have some bad news. It's about your granddaughter, Delilah." Det. Nilo began, but by her reaction, Nilo could tell she already knew.

"Yes." Ms. Brown's voice cracked. "My baby is dead. Oh, my God. Jesus. Lord!" Ms. Brown broke down in the detective's arms.

In situations like this, Det. Nilo was very careful in how he handled the victim's grieving family. He knew it was best to just take his time and console the old woman. He had handled many cases where the victim's family turned against the investigating detectives. That made the case harder to solve.

"Ma'am." Det. Nilo said softly. "I feel your pain. Death is a tough thing to accept. We can't bring her back, but with your help, we can catch whoever did this."

Ms. Brown's sadness transformed into rage. "Just like last time, just like ya'll caught my daughter's killer!" She screamed. "I heard that story before. My granddaughter is dead. She was only eighteen years old and she's dead. Get the hell outta my house harassing me. Go do your job!"

Det. Scott sat down next to Ms. Brown and her eyes quickly averted to him. He was a tall, thin black man with a goatee.

"I'm sorry Ma'am. I know this is a difficult time for you, but there never is any good time for something like this." Det. Scott paused to let his words sink in. When they appeared to be, he continued. "We really need to know if there is anyone that you know of that may have wanted to hurt your granddaughter."

Tears streamed down Ms. Brown's face. "My baby was an angel. She wouldn't hurt a soul. Why would anyone want to hurt her? On the news, they said there was a car accident. Why do you think someone killed her?"

Det. Nilo sighed. "All three bodies, I mean people, in the vehicle had gunshot wounds to the head. This is a fact we're withholding from the media for as long as we can."

"A bullet wound? No, No, No! She was only 18! Oh God, please give me strength." Ms. Brown supplicated with shaking hands. "Why couldn't I have been there? Why? It's all my fault."

Det. Scott gently took her by the hand. "No it's not your fault. There are some sick people in this world, and no matter how much we care, some still want to hate. It's not your fault, but we do need your help. Is there anything you can tell us that might help our investigation?"

Ms. Brown shook her head, wiping her eyes. "She never told me about any problems. She loved to sing. She was so sweet. Please, find my baby's killer."

Det. Scott dropped his head and sighed, then handed her his card. "Here's my numbers. You can reach me there anytime, night or day. If you think of or hear anything, give me a call, please. I'd appreciate it a great deal." Det. Scott

rose from the couch.

"Our deepest sympathies to you and your family,

ma'am. Goodnight." Det. Nilo added, and the two detectives

went out the door.

As they descended the steps, Nilo had to ask. "Hey

Scott, this address isn't in the file we got, how'd you know

where she lived?"

Just like a cop, Scott thought, then said. "I used to

live around here remember. I told you that earlier. Besides, I

was also a beat cop on these same streets. It's no secret that

Delilah's grandma lived in this building."

Nilo shrugged it off as they got in the car.

Oblivious to almost everything around her, the old

woman never saw them leave. She just looked up one minute

and they were gone. Nevertheless, she was glad that they had

left. She didn't want to show her weakness around strangers.

How she prayed this wasn't reality. It was just too painful to accept that it was real and that Delilah was gone.

Murdered? Who on earth could hurt such a sweet delicate flower? Delilah never hurt anyone. She didn't have any enemies. She was a very special girl that very few people really knew. They only knew Delilah the entertainer, but she knew the real flesh and blood, she knew her heart.

At this point, death didn't seem so bad to Ms. Brown. Life had suddenly become too hard for her to deal with. She swore she was cursed, as if she had a bad karma surrounding her. She felt lifeless without her granddaughter, as if life wasn't worth living anymore. She bore the brunt of one too many harsh blows from living. In the past, she had weathered the storm. This time she feared that she didn't have the will power to bounce back.

Death had such finality to it, she wouldn't wish this kind of pain and suffering on her worst enemy. There was no coming back from it. When you are gone, you're gone. It still didn't seem real. This could not have happened to Delilah. She prayed for her baby every night. She did everything she possibly could to keep her safe. She loved Delilah for who she was, not the fortune, fame or the public persona that surrounded her. Right now she would trade all her granddaughter's success just to have her back, amongst the living. Melinda raised that little princess like her own and now she was gone.

As she sat on the bed, wallowing in her misery and reminiscing over the times she and her granddaughter shared, suddenly a light flipped on inside of her head. The suitcase! Delilah had told her to keep it in case anything happened to her. The child must have known something was wrong. She was afraid. Melinda wanted to kick herself for not remembering.

Sometimes it was just so hard for her to remember things, with her being in the early stages of Alzheimer's disease. She usually wrote things down, but eventually she found herself forgetting where she left her notepad. Delilah had constantly offered to get her a health assistant, but Melinda wanted to stay independent for as long as possible. Though she didn't dare admit it, deep down inside Melinda knew that she didn't have much longer before something had to give. The day was rapidly approaching where she would need help doing the normal things able-bodied people tend to take for granted.

Immediately, she knew where she had placed the suitcase. At least she thought she did. Did I place it in the hallway closet? Or maybe my room closet? Yeah, it's in my room closet, she concluded to herself. Then slowly, she hobbled off her bed, heading to her closet to retrieve the suitcase. Confidently, she pushed aside the sliding closet doors, and then she moved around old heavy winter garments, til the suitcase finally came in sight. Melinda breathed a huge sigh of relief, she had found what she was desperately searching for. Bless the Lord, there it was. Her memory hadn't completely failed her.

Struggling to remove the suitcase from the closet, Melinda had to wrestle it away from the fallen clothes. After dragging the suitcase from the closet over to her bed, she finally was able to rest the bulky thing on her lap. Slowly she opened it, as if something inside would jump out at her. Quietly, she said a silent prayer. She hoped she would not discover anything that would shed a negative light on her granddaughter's life. She hoped there was nothing inside the suitcase she shouldn't know about, nothing that would bring her shame. A tear slowly escaped her eye as she opened the suitcase. She caught a whiff of Delilah's perfume that immediately made her miss her little baby.

"I can't do this." She thought, as she slammed the suitcase shut. Maybe she should just give it to the detectives. Let them snoop through it. Maybe they could come up with some clues.

Come on Melinda, she thought. This is what your granddaughter wanted. Melinda decided to be strong and have faith in the Lord. She had long passed the threshold of suffering that she could mortally endure. It was only God who was caring for her now. She slowly reopened the suitcase.

Detective Nilo looked at himself in the mirror as he shaved. Delilah Brown. To him, it was no big deal. Besides the fact that she had been murdered, which was a crime, there was no reason in particular to get worked up just because she was a singer. Everywhere he turned, there were eulogies and dedications to the slain entertainer, and personally he was tired of it. It wasn't like she was Frank Sinatra, Nilo pondered. Now that was a singer. People didn't flip out when he passed. Just another testament to Nilo that the world was going to hell in a hand basket.

To Nilo, Delilah was just a victim of circumstance. All these rappers out here, threatening each other in their songs and shooting at each other didn't make any sense to him, and he would bet his bottom dollar that whoever killed her probably had something to do with that lifestyle. After all, her boyfriend was a rapper who was just involved in a shooting. If she hadn't been famous, this would be a back page case and Delilah would be just another dead black girl. But Nilo had dedicated himself to the case for another reason entirely. He could feel the plush seat cushion of the captain's chair. After he solved this big case, he'd definitely be a shoe in. Or just maybe, he could run for Borough President or even Mayor. If these people loved Delilah Brown so much, let their love boost his career all the way to the top. He'd be their hero, when in actuality, he was just an ambitious detective.

Det. Scott had slept at his desk. He spent the night pouring over the different angles and leads. Most led nowhere. These he wouldn't worry about. He knew where he would have to concentrate his efforts. There was enough scandal in the music industry these days to find a motive for

anything, including murder. It was just a matter of time and

he'd have this case wrapped up. Unlike Nilo, he wasn't

looking for a captain's position or borough election, he just

wanted closure in this case. Why did she have to die? He

asked himself over and over. She was young and beautiful,

with the world at her feet. But then again, that in itself is

reason enough for murder. If it's lonely at the top, that's only

because you can't trust anyone on the come up. Everybody

wants a piece of you.

Scott remembered seeing Delilah around the

neighborhood, but he mostly recalled the first time he had

really interacted with her on a personal level. He had been a

beat cop in the Bronx and was assigned as security to Tower

Records for her album signing. People milled around

everywhere. The line outside was a mile long in anticipation

for her arrival. Unlike a lot of stars, she wasn't late and he

could tell she wanted to please her fans. Delilah stepped

from the stretch limo wearing a pink leather skirt set that complimented her flawless legs. Those brown toned works of art were the first thing he saw of the young vixen, but it was her smile that had him captured. He watched her the entire afternoon mingling with fans, signing autographs, giving hugs and taking pictures. She never appeared fake or put off by their exuberance.

Scott had never been good with women, despite his height and boy next door good looks. He was clean cut and polite, but it seemed the women in his life weren't attracted to good guys. His last girlfriend had been a close friend coming out of an abusive relationship, and he had been there for her, boosting her self-esteem and nursing her emotions back to good health. Three months later, she left him with the same type of broken heart she came to him with.

Scott glanced at his watch and knew Nilo would be there soon. They had a case to solve and Scott vowed to himself that he'd do his best to bring closure. For himself and the rest of the grieving city.

Slowly, Ms. Brown again peeked into her granddaughter's mysterious suitcase. As she did so, her heart began to race like a cardiac patient. Suddenly tears started down her leathery bronze cheeks. The first tear seemed to open a floodgate of pain, she began to sob uncontrollably, and soon her face turned pale and her eyes bloodshot red. Silently, she prayed to God Almighty, calling on her Lord to give her strength.

Her granddaughter's death was so surreal. Though she knew the news reports were true, she drifted in and out of a state of denial. The tidal wave of phone calls from her church congregation, condolences, and well-wishers had helped her retain her sanity.

Still she felt as if somebody had to pay for this, one way or another. Who would want to hurt Delilah?

Ms. Brown ruffled through the contents of the suitcase. There was a makeup kit, some dancing shoes, and a black and white composition notebook. Her curiosity was magnetically pulled to the notebook. She lifted it out of the suitcase and stared at the cover. The book seemed to be at least a couple years old. A thin coat of dust had settled on it, and from the beat up condition it was in, obviously it had been hidden. Melinda's eyes were captivated by the bold print on the cover. In a youthful, sloppy scrawl, were the words: *The Life and Times of Delilah Brown, Pop Diva.*

The old woman's weary eyes canvassed the cover over and over. She could feel her granddaughter's presence all over the small notebook. She had an awkward clammy feeling in the pit of her stomach. There was a familiar sensation of heat across her chest. Melinda remembered this feeling from a very long time ago, the empty day she lost Felicia. The solemn grandmother opened the book. She struggled to ease on her reading glasses with one hand, then stared at the first page. Melinda thought about the dangerous atmospheres that Delilah must have found herself in. That whole music business was so superficial and money hungry. It was definitely a dog eat dog world. Melinda braced herself for any details about Delilah's life that she cared not to know. Nevertheless, she began to read.

October 12th

Hey ya'll, my name is Delilah Brown, as if you didn't know. I am eighteen years old. Naw, I'm frontin'! I'ma keep it real. Ya'll know how that go. Every teenager is in a rush to be 18. But my birthday is next week. (Can't wait either.) That's whutz up. I'm just chillin.' My home girl, Jenny told me the other day that she thought I lived the most interesting life that she could ever imagine. She said that my life could be a movie or something. Imagine that. So anyway, I decided to document this part of my life.

For two reasons: 1) To give outsiders an up close and personal look at the real me, not the person you see on TV.

46

2) Just in case anything goes down, people would know what I was about. Anyway, I'm gonna be writing in this journal from time to time, to express myself or to get some stress off my chest. Just whenever I can. My therapist, well, I don't go no more, but I used to go when I was younger. She said that it was a good thing to write your thoughts down, so maybe this will help.

Anyway, I'm an R&B singer. (A damn good one too, if I might add.) Some people might say that I'm well known or famous. I saw in one of those magazines that they called me a Pop Diva. I couldn't fuckin' believe it. I almost cried. But anyway, I am really living out my dream, touring, doing shows, making some money, and just doing what I love. How many people can truly say that? Huh? I love my job!

Okay, well I am on the set of my new video, "Take Me There". It is a beautiful song that I wrote back when I was in the seventh grade. So anyway, I gotta go get fly. Image is everything in this business. The hairdresser is waving at me like a mad man, or madwoman. I think he's gay, whatever

though. That's on him! Gotta jet. I'll get back at you in a

few. One love D-Nice!!

Melinda smiled brightly. This was the innocent
grandchild she knew. Her words had expertly captured her
simple child like state. Delilah had such a love for life. She
was the type of person who could just light up a room. She
approached everything with a down-to-earth humility that
was almost childlike. Melinda's eyes began to water. She
decided to turn the page and keep reading.

December 18th

Yo, what up world? What's really good? This ya girl,

Delilah once again. Yo, I haven't written in awhile. I've been

crazy busy doing this promotional tour. I can't complain,

beats bein' on the block. I performed on a bunch of TV

shows, signed autographs, did crazy interviews, and all that

good stuff. Sometimes it's hard to believe that people

actually wanna interview me! I ain't nobody for real for

real!! Just a poor little black girl from the Bronx. I ain't on like that, just cause I sing. Na! But half the muthafuckin' industry is stuck on themselves. They act like they walk on water or somethin'. It hurts me to see how they really are, and I used to idolize a lot of them cats too. That's on them. I'm still me, and I hope and pray I never change. Gotta stay grounded, the same people you meet on the way up, is the same ones you see on the way down. A little girl got an autograph from me in the mall and she started crying. I was like, what? I really feel dumb sometimes. It's almost like a dream, like it's not real. Can't believe I'm touching people like that. But my girl Jenny says this is just the beginning. I'm about to be crazy large. I believe her too.

Speaking of her, she always keep it real. She don't pull no punches. It is, what it is, with her. We have been friends since the fourth grade. Now, when I tell you that me and that girl have been through some stuff, I mean we really, really been through some stuff, ya feel me! We had another so-called friend named Sasha. But she ain't rollin' wit us no more cause she's a hater, and that's bein' nice. She hates me cause, when we got put on, they decided to put just me on instead of the whole group. It's a long story. Well see, all three of us was up on 125th doing some shoppin' (very little because we were broke, we were really window shopping). Anyway, Sasha had on these Daisy Duke short shorts that had her ass hangin' out. She was lookin' like a slut for real. Although she always wear tight shit, this day she outdid herself. Gotta give her her props, she do got a helluva body. Her titties stand at attention and her ass is ridiculously fat. And I ain't gay either, but it is what it is. So yeah, she stocked, but her grill, well, that's a whole different story. Let's just say, she ain't no beauty queen. She ain't ugly, but she ain't pretty either. God forgive me for backbiting. I feel so bad for saying that.

So bust it, this fly ass Benz pulled up bumpin' Cam'ron, but I ain't really pay it no mind cause 125th always be packed wit sick whips. That is, until the driver got out and stepped to Sasha. But when she turned around, well, we already discussed her grill. Then he saw me. I ain't gonna front, KB had it goin' on and then some. Smooth ass brown skin, chinky eyes, and his body, oh my God, this nigga was ripped up like the Hulk. So, he definitely had my attention, but I ain't let him know that cause I ain't want him to think I was sweatin' him, especially with the way Sasha was acting after she saw he was all on me and not her.

So yo, we kicked it and he took all of us shopping. Well really me, but I begged him to buy Jenny and Sasha something, which he did. He seemed real nice. I say seemed, because well, we'll get into all that later. At first, it wasn't all that serious, but then I really started diggin' KB cause we could talk about anything. I even told him that we wanted to be singers. He ain't believe we could sing, but when we did, his mouth dropped and he told me he could introduce us to Big Rock. Now KB had mad respect because he was a hustler and official gangster. But Big Rock? The number one rapper in the world? I didn't think so, not until we found ourselves up in Rock's midtown Manhattan studio singing our little hearts out.

We were like wow, Big Rock! We were true star struck fans. He was the man in the rap game! We sang for Big Rock, but when he called the next week, he only wanted me. At first I was like no way, but then I realized that if they were really my friends, they would support me. It was kind of rough because we all had this big dream for us to make it together. We would sit in front of the TV, watching videos, award shows, singing at talent shows and all that. I hated to leave my girls behind, but it was my only shot. Jenny was cool about it. She stayed by my side, thank God. I love her and I need her so much in my life. Now Sasha, on the other hand, she won't even talk to us. But one day, maybe one day, she'll get her mind right and stop hatin'. That's on her though, either way, I ain't mad at her. I'm too busy takin' care of business. Ya heard! Enough said, looking at my

Gucci, it's about that time. I'm out! See ya when I see ya! I'll

holla back soon. This writing shit is starting to get fun. It

brings back mad old memories! I really wish things coulda

turned out differently though. But it's not my plan, it's God's

plan. One Luv. C-ya! D-Nice.

Detectives Nilo and Scott drove downtown in deep silence, both lost in their own thoughts. Their destination was Intersound Entertainment, Delilah's record company headquarters. They maneuvered through heavily congested blocks of New York traffic to get to Intersound's Time Square recording studio. Once there, they hoped to find Intersound's Chairman, Tito Diez, who was on top of a long list of Delilah's friends and associates that were possible suspects.

Intersound's headquarters were located in a nondescript building. It was in between two fast food restaurants. To the detectives, it seemed that nothing of importance could possibly take place there. If only they knew this was Hit-Ville, U.S.A.. This was the place where most of the hit R&B records that dominated the radio airwaves, were made. This was the place stars were born. To say that the location was modest, would be an understatement.

One look at the place, from the outside, and the detectives feared they were in the wrong spot. Upon entering the building and looking at the directory, their fears were calmed. There it was plain as day, Intersound Entertainment, 16th floor. The two-man detective team moved fluently and swiftly through the hallway of the building lobby, as if they were one. They were on a mission. They were well-seasoned veterans, having worked countless homicide cases. Meticulous at investigating, they left no stone unturned.

Catching the first available elevator, they rode it up to the 16th floor in dead silence. Exiting the elevator, the two detectives walked through two thick glass doors, with gold colored door handles. Behind it in bold block letters, hung a three-dimensional sign, 'INTERSOUND ENT'.

A beautiful young bleach blonde Puerto Rican secretary sat in front of the logo, at a large oval wooden desk. Their sudden appearance somewhat startled her, and upon closer inspection, she knew that they were the police. To her, they had cops written all over them.

It was beginning to be the norm, Rap and R&B labels were being thoroughly investigated by the F.B.I for possible links to illicit drug trades and money laundering. Several record labels had already been raided, financial records and computers had been seized, even record label assets and bank accounts were frozen. She knew it was only a matter of time before the Feds came sniffing around there. Reaching under her desk, she buzzed them in.

"Whut'z good Officers? What brings you here? Looking for somebody or whut?" The burly security guard asked, as he defiantly stood blocking the entrance to the record company. He stood right next to the secretary's desk, eagerly stroking his gun. He was just a rapper's homeboy, recently released from prison. On the strength of his muscular physical build, he was given a job as security.

Det. Scott pulled his badge out of his coat pocket. "Police business. Please step aside sir." He said calmly.

Briefly the two men, from different sides of the tracks, locked eyes. They glared menacingly at each other, as if at any given moment a fight could erupt. Having second thoughts, the bodyguard backed down, looking away. Reluctantly, he obeyed the command turning his body ever so slightly, barely allowing enough room for the detectives to pass.

Offended, Det. Scott immediately took this as a sign of disrespect, feeling the man was trying to show him up in front of his partner.

"You got one fuckin' second to move ya fat ass out the way, before I lock your big dumb ass up!" Det. Scott barked. "You hear me?"

The vulgar language got the desired effect, as the security guard moved completely out of the way. As he passed, Det. Scott made sure to roughly bump the man with his shoulder. He tried to further humiliate him.

Having witnessed the strong verbal reprimand, the secretary decided to handle the two police officers with finesse. "Hello, officers. How may I help you?" She inquired politely.

"Umm, yes." Det. Scott replied. "We're looking for a Tito Diez. Is he in?"

"And whom shall I say is here?"

"Detectives Scott and Nilo. Homicide." They seemed to say in unison.

"Just one moment gentlemen. Would you please be seated?" She said. The secretary got up from her plush black leather chair and disappeared down a long hallway.

Det. Scott openly admired the lovely figure, seductively strutting in her form fitting skirt. In amazement, he stared at her behind until she was out of eyesight. Breaking out into a sly grin, he looked at his partner as if to say. "Did you see that?" Then he began shaking his head from side to side, in appreciation of her sexy shape.

Almost on cue, they both sat down on opposite ends of a long, luxurious black leather couch. Patiently they waited, giving Mr. Diez every chance to play fair, to meet with them face-to-face. Before they even knew it, twenty minutes had passed and still no sign of the head honcho. Det. Scott wondered quietly to himself. "Was there some secret exit in the building, a trap door or a back way out? Were they stalling for time while he fled?" He had just begun to give that notion some serious thought when the sexy secretary suddenly reappeared.

"I'm sorry to inform you, but Mr. Diez is not available at this time. He has very important business matters he needs to address. So, if you detectives don't have an arrest warrant, I'll have to ask you to leave the premises. If there are any problems, you can talk to Mr. Diez's attorney. Good day detectives. Would you please step right this way?" She said.

"Oh, yeah?" Det. Nilo snapped. "We'll talk to his lawyer alright. C'mon partner! We're gonna pay the scum bag a visit."

Bypassing the beautiful Puerto Rican secretary, the detectives made a beeline straight towards Mr. Diez's office.

"Hey, wait a minute! Where do you think you're going?" She screamed. "Do you hear me? Ya'll can't just barge in there like that! This is private property! Ya'll about to get sued for this shit! That's illegal!" The secretary yelled in vain, but she was physically powerless to stop them.

Ignoring her warnings, they cautiously continued moving down the hallway. As they did so, they passed multiple platinum and gold plaques. The secretary persisted in her yelling, forcing Det. Nilo to stop and cause an unwanted commotion with his response back to her.

"Just shut ya big mouth and do ya fuckin' job lady. This is between us men. Don't worry ya pretty self over it. And don't get any funny ideas about bein' brave and try to stop us either. You'll be locked down on Riker's Island. Those ugly ass bull dykes over there would have a ball with you, I can see it now. Seriously, I suggest you back off." Det. Nilo warned.

"Miss, if I were you, I'd heed his warning. He doesn't like to repeat himself. Just do what you do best, look pretty." Det. Scott suggested, as if he were trying to save the young lady a whole lot of grief.

The secretary wisely complied with him. She sat down quietly, with her bottom lip poked out as if she were a small child who had just been disciplined.

After putting the young lady in her place, the detectives continued on their way, snooping as they went along. Soon, the strong scent of marijuana assaulted their nostrils. Without warning, a few feet away a door suddenly flung open. Quickly Det. Nilo grabbed his partner's arm, alerting him to the possibility of danger up ahead. They quickly assessed the potential threat, and concluded it was no threat at all.

Two young black males, engrossed in a private conversatin, walked unknowingly towards them. As one kid passed the marijuana to the next, they suddenly spotted them and immediately their cop radar went off. In their neighborhood, they were trained at a young age how to identify a cop. This went hand in hand with the territory. After cleverly cuffing the marijuana filled cigar, known as a blunt, they smoothly reversed directions, heading back into the room they had just come out of. The detectives didn't bother to harass them, they were well beyond busting young thugs for smoking weed. That was for rookies, plainclothes cops and overzealous beat walkers.

Walking a few feet further, they finally found what they were looking for. Painted on a door, was a large gold Hollywood star, underneath in cursive letters, a name was nicely written. It read Tito Diez, CEO, Intersound Entertainment. The detectives drew their weapons, preparing for whatever lay in wait for them on the other side of the door. On each side of the door they held a strategic position, and on the silent count of three they burst through the door.

Mr. Diez had been on the phone, in the middle of an important business deal, when suddenly his office door flew open. Cautiously entering the room, the detectives waved their guns from side to side, at any would be attackers.

Walking over to Tito, Det. Nilo abruptly snatched the phone out of his hand, forcefully hanging it up.

"Oh, shit!" Tito managed to say. The bewildered look in his eyes, showed the presence of fear that his face didn't. "What the fuck?"

"Fun times over, pretty boy!" He announced. "We got a few questions to ask you."

Not one to judge another man, even Det. Nilo had to admit that Tito Diez was an incredibly handsome man. His strong European features betrayed his Hispanic last name. It was quite clear to the detectives that Tito was anything but Spanish. His facial features suggested otherwise, especially the olive tone complexion. It spoke volumes of his Italian heritage. He probably adopted his stage name to make himself more acceptable to his predominately minority colleagues and to give himself more street credibility in the hood.

Besides being blessed with flawless physical features, Tito was also a very well dressed man. Probably one, if not the best, dressed man in the music industry. The chairman's Armani slacks and Maury shoes complimented the Presidential Rolex on his wrist. He had class and money written all over him. He carried himself with an air of importance.

From the moment he laid eyes on him, Det. Nilo couldn't stand the sight of Tito Diez. He couldn't stand rich people period, especially entertainers and athletes. To him, they thought they owned the world. When, in all actuality, they had been unfairly placed on pedestals, looked up to as role models, when the average every day people were the real heroes, people like him. Let them try working a nine to five and all the overtime they could get, just to put food on the table and put two kids through college. Maybe then they would appreciate the true value of a hard day's work.

"What the fuck you two think ya doin'?" Tito protested, putting up a brave front. "Do you know this is against the law? The same law you've sworn to protect. It's called breaking and entering. By the way, do you realize who the hell I am? My attorney is gonna have both ya asses on a silver platter for this shit. By the time he's through with you two, ya'll be directing traffic in West Bubba Fuck somewhere. You hear me?"

"Oh really? You heard that partner?" Det. Scott smartly remarked. "This gentleman is issuing threats to us. Can you imagine that? Ooooh, look I'm real scared. Partner you scared too?"

The two detectives let out long exaggerated bursts of laughter. Then suddenly they flipped the script.

"Look you fuckin' clown!" Det. Scott continued, pointing his index finger in his face. "A very talented and beautiful young lady was killed yesterday. And we're the investigating officers. This is a very high profile case. The fuckin' Chief of Police and even the damn Mayor himself is breathing down our backs to solve this case quickly. So we didn't just randomly select your name out of a hat or something. We're conducting a very thorough investigation here, looking at all possible links to the victim. We asked politely to get a few moments of your time, but you didn't respect that. You sent one of your flunkies to run us away. Now talk about a slap in the face? So now that we've got your complete undivided attention, we need to ask you a few questions. We can do this the easy way or the hard way. It's on you. Whichever you prefer is fine with us. Just make it easy on yourself."

At that precise moment, Tito realized he was in a no-win situation. These detectives looked like they meant business. They were going to get the information out of him, one way or another, even if it meant a little police brutality. After calculating the risk in his head, he decided it was in his best interest to cooperate with the authorities. He figured, why add insult to injury?

"Well, what do you wanna know detectives?" Tito questioned. "My guess is as good as yours at this point. Quite honestly, I think ya'll barkin' up the wrong tree. But I guess ya'll gotta job to do though. Me, for one, I don't see where I could be of any real help to ya'll. Still ya'll ain't convinced of my innocence, no matter what I say. Everybody is a suspect, questions need to be asked. I'm ready. Now c'mon shoot!"

"Alright, if you insist Mr. Diez. That's the attitude, pretend we one of ya homies, let's just kick it, as they say. Now let's take it from the top. Tell us about your relationship with the late Delilah Brown? What exactly, if any, was your role in her life?"

Lowering his head, Tito ran both his hands through his jet black, slicked back hair, as if this act would release some of the unwanted stress he was feeling. Taking a deep

breath, he exhaled loudly, then began to speak.

"Delilah Brown was good people. She never played

nobody. She was one beautiful human being, inside and out.

They don't make 'em like that no more. Damn shame, a

tragedy how she died. She didn't deserve to go out like that.

Really, it's hard to believe she's gone. Just the other day, she

stopped by and we kicked it for a while. We talked about

everything, laughing and joking like crazy. I didn't just lose

my number one recording artist, I lost a good friend. True

friends only come around once in a lifetime. Now to add

insult to injury, you two are trying to point the finger at me.

Ya'll come busting down my fuckin' door, no warrant or

nuttin', like I did it or something. Aint that some shit?"

"Wait a minute." Det. Nilo cautioned. "We never

accused you of anything. Maybe you got a guilty conscious

or something. If you're as innocent as you say, then you have

nothing to hide or worry about."

"You're absolutely right. Ya'll just gimme a funny feeling. Sometimes evidence has a way of being found in the most convenient places, and nobody knows how it got there, if you catch my drift."

"I'm offended." Det. Scott exclaimed, faking like his feelings were hurt. "Det. Nilo, if I didn't know better, I'd believe he just called us crooked cops."

"No, our friend wouldn't bad mouth us like that." Det. Nilo announced. "Would you Tito?"

"Of course not." He added, playing along. "I wasn't talking about you two. Just repeating what I heard. Shit happens."

"Well, we don't do that kind of shit. We don't have to. In the end, we always get our man, understand? Now stick to the script."

"Like I was saying, Delilah was well liked within the music industry and worshipped by her fans. She had the looks to match her talent too. One of my rappers was on her like stink on shit."

"Besides the puppy love, did she have any enemies? Any business deals gone wrong? Any beef with rival singers on different labels?" Det. Scott questioned.

"Not that I know of." He replied.

"Well, how was her financial standing here at the label?" Det. Scott probed. "Was she making money?"

"Hell yeah! Delilah wasn't hurting by a long shot on the money side of things. She was well on her way to becoming a millionaire."

The two detectives exchanged a satisfied look, as if to say this is enough. "Okay, if anything else comes up, we'll be in touch, here's my card. Mr. Diez. if you see or hear anything, give me a holler."

Diez's sweaty hand gripped the card. "No problem detective. I gotcha."

"Our condolences." Det. Scott whispered. Then the two detectives turned and left his office.

"That guy is lying through his teeth." Det. Nilo told his partner, once outside. "Why don't we run downtown and get the okay for twenty-four hour surveillance wire taps, the works? I gotta feelin' he is not tellin' us everything."

Chapter 3

Melinda stared into empty space for a few seconds. She was so confused. She had to gather her thoughts. The phone was ringing non-stop off of the hook, but she decided to ignore it. Her shaky hand continued to turn the page. She felt a tinkle of cold air sweep across the room. To her it was much more than a chill, she felt the presence of a spirit. It was as if her deceased granddaughter was watching over her. She shook off the fear that had suddenly gripped her, knowing Delilah's spirit would do her no harm. She buttoned up her sweater and cuddled close to the pillows on the loveseat. She sighed sadly and continued to read.

February 15th

Hey young world. It's me, ya girl, Delilah. Holla!
What's really good? What the deal? Me, I'm just chillin'.
Everything is still everything. I just got back from the
Grammy's. That's one of the main reasons I ain't been
writing too much. Been mad busy. Anyway, I won eight
awards! Can you believe it? That shit was crazy! For real!
Who would have thought the kid woulda won that many
awards. On the real, not me! I was dumb nervous each time I
was nominated. I couldn't believe how they kept hollerin' my
name! Hearin' my name called sent chills down my spine.
That definitely fucked my head up. I was shocked! Even
though I knew that I was up for a lot of awards, each time
they called my name, it felt just as good as the first time! I
have never, never felt so proud in all my life. I really shined
that night. I just wish my grandmother wasn't so shook of

74

flying, she coulda been there too, holdin' me down. Instead, it was just me, Rock, his crew, and Jenny. Jenny's my peoples, but I wish my blood was there too. Anyway, Rock didn't win nothing and he was tight like a muthafucka too. He just knew that he was takin' home a grammy. So, when he didn't, he was real salty. Anyway, I really thought he would have been at least happy for me. I mean, if the shoe were on the other foot, I woulda been happy for him. Guess everybody don't think like that? Huh? I think that he was hatin' on the down low though. He only told me congratulations one time and that was it. You could tell he didn't even mean it. Jenny said he was jealous, actin' like a real bitch! But she don't even know the whole story. There is a lot going on between me and him right now. It's a long story. I guess I gotta start from the beginning.

See when I first met Big Rock, I was so shook. I could have peed on myself. I was scared to death. He was this big rap star. And I was a nothing, a nobody, basically just a big fan. When we sang for him, he just kept starin' at me. Yo, I was only sixteen but I never looked my age. People always told me that. I ain't fast, hot in the pants, conceited or anything like that, but I know I look crazy good, even to older niggas. He was feelin' me, no doubt, I can tell when a nigga sweatin' me. Still, I couldn't believe it though. The nigga could have had his pick of women, chicks, groupies, hoes and freaks, but he wanted to get wit me. Of course, he played it off like he wasn't payin' me no mind. Like this was strictly business. Like he don't mix work wit play. He was so professional and everything, you know. I was definitely flattered, but I already was fuckin' wit somebody anyway. You know, I had a man and Big Rock knew that. Remember KB?

That was my heart. I dug everything bout him, from the way he walked, to the way he talked. And he had the most perfect teeth, framed in the most perfect set of full lips. He was so fine and so sexy, it wasn't even funny. On top of that, he was cock diesel. He was cut up like a bag of dope. He had

big arms and abs. Basically, the nigga had a body to die for!

When I went round his way, I noticed people treated me wit

so much respect on the strength of him. In no time, I was

open off him. He had crazy game, had my head gassed up on

some bullshit. To hear him tell it, I was his only shorty, his

wifey and he wasn't fuckin' wit nobody else, to hear him tell

it. I was so stupid, I ate that shit right up. He could do no

wrong in my eyes.

Seems like right after we fucked, things started to

change, for the worse. Basically, he started playin' me out,

cheatin' and shit. Then he'd flip out when he got caught. He

would get real rough with me sometimes. He'd smack me or

push me when we would argue. At first, I thought it was my

fault, but then I realized he was a woman beater. I found out

the nigga was into all kinds of illegal shit. He kept crazy

guns in his crib. All the dirt he was doin' in the streets finally

caught up to his dumb ass. He eventually got busted by the

Feds. He got caught up in an undercover gun buy and bust operation. He was facin' crazy time too, cause the Feds, don't play. So now, he wanna be that good nigga, promising me he gonna change when he come home. I felt sorry for him, and went to see him in jail a couple of times, but after the whole Big Rock thing, his prison homies started gettin' in his head. He saw me on a video with Big Rock and totally flipped out on me. He started calling me from jail and threatening me and shit. He said he was gonna kill me if I left him. If he couldn't have me, then nobody would. He kept asking me crazy questions 'bout Big Rock, asking me if I was fuckin' him now. Now, me and Aaron, that's Big Rock's real name, we wasn't even doin' nuttin' for real. We flirted with each other now and then, but that was it. Like the time when we were recording the album and doin' the video, but I never cheated on KB. If he would have kept it real, I would have waited for him. No question. But Jenny found out about a couple of those chicken heads he had been messin' wit behind my back. I even think that he was still messin' 'round wit Sasha on the low.

Outta nowhere, he started to get crazy jealous, trying to control me, calling me, telling me he was gonna kill me. He was really stressin' me out, I was throwing up every day, I lost 'bout fifteen pounds. The only person I could turn to at that time was Big Rock. My grandmother definitely wouldn't be able to understand. She was too old fashioned. Jenny would just overreact and blow shit out of proportion. That would make me even more stressed out. Big Rock was such a gentleman. He never pushed me to do anything I didn't want to do. He was the perfect medium between the two. He didn't try to make a move on me even at one of the worst points of my life. I never thought I would get involved wit a rapper or anyone involved in the industry because of all the temptation, all the groupies and stuff. But never say never. Shit happens! I thought he wasn't the average nigga.

I'll never forget the day that he told me he wanted us to hook up. In front of everybody, he said that I was his girl and it was all 'bout me and him from now on. That felt crazy good. Big Rock bought me everything, minks, designer shoes and bags, he went all out. Money wasn't a thing to Big Rock. We were in the newspapers and magazines. He made me feel like we were Jennifer Lopez and P. Diddy. He was so different than KB. He knew what to say to me, how to touch me, he was just on another level. I can't explain how safe and secure I felt wit him. KB would just fuck me and get up. He was such a selfish lover. Big Rock took his time, he worked me. He would look at my body in amazement, like I was the finest woman that he had ever laid eyes on. It seemed like he appreciated me. Even though KB kept mailing me threatening letters and calling me, I still felt safe wit Aaron, I mean Big Rock. Plus my girl, Jenny got along with him, it was all good. He even helped produce my first album for me. He made sure the beats were hot and the songs were arranged perfectly, so that my album would be a smash hit.

He handpicked all of the producers. He also helped take care

of the business side of things with Jenny, telling her things

she had no clue about. All I had to do was sing and that's

how I wanted it. Everything was straight. I was really

starting to fall in love with Big Rock.

I thought I loved KB, but I realized that it wasn't love

at all, it was lust. Big Rock made me feel like no other. For

the first time I was really happy. Every now and then I would

see little signs of him cheating. I would find some numbers,

but I just overlooked it, I knew I had him. He cared about me

and I convinced myself that was all that mattered. But me

and him started having some problems cause of a secret that

I kept from him. It was burnin' inside of me, but once I felt

that he cared enough for me not to leave me once he knew, I

told him (listening to Jenny stupid-ass). It's a long story, but

I'll try to make it short because I gotta go shopping wit

Jenny, then I gotta meet wit my publicist.

So anyway, after I first sang for Big Rock, he took me up to his record company, Intersound Records. He took me into the Chairman's office. His name was Tito Diez. At first I was callin' him Mr. Diez, but he told me to just call him Tito. This guy was filthy rich and he was a real, I mean, real handsome and intelligent type of guy. He told Rock that he only had a few minutes to hear me sing cuz his private jet was waiting to take him to lunch with some congressman. This cat was so smooth. I mean he was real serious and so powerful looking. So, I sang for him. I was crazy nervous. At first, I was embarrassed cuz when I finished, he didn't say anything, he just stared at me. Then his phone rang and he answered it. Once he hung up his phone, he said goodbye to the both of us and then left. Big Rock told me that means he liked me. And sure enough, he called Big Rock a few hours later and told him to sign me immediately. I was like wow! They signed me for seven years. I got like a half a million dollar budget to do my first album. Big Rock got most of that money for producer fees, but that's a different story.

Okay, I'm runnin late now so I'll get to the point. A week later, there was a brand new Mercedes Benz with a big red ribbon wrapped around it outside of my grandmother's building. There was a note attached that said. "Call me, Tito. So you know I called him. Of course, this was before me and Big Rock got together. Anyway, he flew me to some beach resort in France. It was like a dream. He told me how he was gonna make me a star. I had maids waiting on me hand and foot. I felt like a Princess. I had never felt that way before. Unfortunately, I made a horrible mistake wit Tito that weekend. I guess I can't really say it was a horrible mistake and I can't say that I totally regret it. It was fun. I knew what I was doing. This may sound crazy, but I kinda liked it. Later I really regretted it though.

KB was my first, and let me tell you, being with Tito that weekend, the difference was amazing! He was the bomb!

That's all I can say. I had never been with a man, I mean a grown ass man before. He touched me with experienced hands, he made me feel weak all over. He took so much time with every touch. I couldn't help but imagine how many hoes he had turned out in his lifetime. With a tongue like his, he was marriage material! His dick was the perfect size, not too small, not too big, but just a perfect fit. But seriously, I knew that it was just physical, and I really didn't give a fuck. It was one of those times when I can truly say that I just wanted to fuck him. I didn't even stop to think about the consequences.

But after we got back, Tito started actin' funny. Me and Big Rock were gettin' close, and I guess that made Tito real jealous. But hell, I found out from a very reliable source (who I won't name), that he was married wit three kids! I can't get involved in that! But anyway, we kind of ended up on bad terms. At times, when I came to the label, he wouldn't even look at me. Of course, he always smiled for the pictures and talked good bout me to the press, but I'll never forget what he told me one time. He said. "You could've had it all, but you wanted to be a little groupie with your rapper boyfriend." I brushed the comment off when he said it, but it really crushed me. I knew that it was all my fault.

But anyway, when I finally told Big Rock what happened, he grabbed me by my neck and slammed me against the wall. He kept yelling. "How could you be such a dumb fuckin' hoe!" His words crushed me. I felt so bad, I really wanted to die right then and there. I had never felt so low in my life. He was right though, I shouldn't have been so stupid. But what was I supposed to do, it was Tito Diez? I kind of figured that maybe, I guess, deep down inside, I had to do this to make it. Or, maybe I just rationalized it to myself that way, I don't know. But anyway, Big Rock stormed out of the house, he hasn't been the same since. Okay, I'm crying now, so I gotta go. I'll holla back soon. - Lilah

Delilah's grandmother was dumbfounded by what she had just read. She stared at the page as if the words somehow changed. That little girl always felt a need to make everybody else happy. Her mom was the same way. It didn't make any sense, you can't be everything to everybody. She hated to find out that her granddaughter was being taken advantage of and used. She started to feel a violent rage exploding inside of her. This was wrong. She wanted to know who killed her granddaughter and why. The phone continued to ring constantly, but she ignored it. She began to notice a rumbling thirst and hunger take over her insides. She ignored that as well. She had to get to the bottom of this. Ms. Brown stretched her weary legs out on the old loveseat and turned the page.

Chapter 4

Detectives Nilo and Scott arrived at their next targeted destination. They had made the troublesome rush hour drive from New York City, across the George Washington Bridge to Fort Lee, New Jersey. Currently, they stood in front of Big Rock's recording studio. Impatiently, Det. Nilo pressed the buzzer on the intercom again, holding it there for a minute.

"Bzzzzzzz!"

A young squeaky voice crackled over the speaker, "Welcome to the Rock House. How may I help you?"

"Police business. Open up!" Det. Nilo scuffed.

"The Rock House, Huh?" Det. Scott shrugged his shoulders and shot him a puzzled look.

"Just some silly rap stuff." Nilo mumbled. "And just think, my son is into all that crap. Hope it's just a faze he's goin' through."

After a loud buzzing sound, the steel front door clicked open. The detectives walked in cautiously. Following a few flights of pale looking stairs, they arrived at yet another security door.

"What is this, fuckin' Fort Knox?" Det. Nilo joked. "Makes you think, what have they got inside that they need so much security?"

After another buzz, they walked into the studio. They were greeted by two huge, bald headed, black men who stood guard on both sides of the entrance.

One of the men stepped towards the detectives. "I'ma need to pat you fellas down. It's company policy, no weapons allowed beyond this point."

Det. Scott looked the security guard up and down and gave him a sarcastic smirk.

"I wish you fuckin' would!" He stated angrily. "It'll be the last thing you ever fuckin' do."

Brandishing his police issued, black nine-millimeter Taurus, Det. Nilo ordered. "Get outta the fuckin' way before I make you a statistic!"

Again, they boldly took the law into their own hands. The two detectives made their way towards the blaring music. The beat was pounding so loudly, that the detectives had to cover their ears.

"These kids are nuts!" Det. Nilo yelled over the music. "Whatever happened to playing music at a sensible level?"

"Tell me about it." Det. Scott agreed. "They'll be hard of hearing in a few years. Then they'll wonder why?"

Before the detectives could enter the studio control room, a young man stepped out. He was slightly muscular, tall and wearing what seemed to be his own body weight in jewels and diamonds. An immense platinum Gucci chain that hung around his neck bore an encrusted emblem that spelled "Big Rock".

"What's the problem Officers?" Big Rock asked politely. "Who ya'll lookin' for?"

"You!" Det. Nilo quickly replied. "You're Big Rock, right? At least that's what that name belt around your neck says. I think you already know what's up and why we are here. But, just in case you don't, let me be the first to inform you. An old girlfriend of yours, Delilah Brown, is dead and we're investigating the case. We need to ask you a few questions. It's just routine procedure."

The young man's face contorted in anger. "Yo, I heard 'bout what happened to shorty, that shit was crazy. But I ain't have nuttin' to do wit it. Why ya'll fuckin' wit me? We been broke up awhile ago. Besides that, I been in this studio all muthafuckin' week working on my next album. I got a least ten witnesses ready to testify for me. So my alibi is airtight. Ya'll ain't gonna railroad me. Not the kid! Especially when I ain't do shit! Na, I ain't goin' out like that. It ain't that type of party."

Det. Nilo shook his head in disgust. "Slow down Rock. You ain't been charged with nothing yet. So save all that legal mumbo jumbo for the judge. We're just here to ask you a few questions, that's all. You can plead the fifth later, so stop jumping the gun."

Big Rock looked relieved. "I was just sayin' though, I ain't tryin to get caught up in that bullshit. A homicide charge ain't nuttin' to play wit."

"We hear ya, Rock." Det. Nilo assured him. "But time's a wasting, let's talk now. Then we both can go about our business. Okay."

Big Rock looked bewildered. "What happened to Delilah? First, I heard she was in a car accident. Now, I'm hearin' she got bodied, I mean murdered."

"Where'd you hear that from?" Det. Scott questioned.

"A very reliable source, the streets. That's the word on the street right now. You know the streets always gets the 411 before anybody else. The streets are always watchin'." Big Rock told them. "Always!"

The man's statement only reaffirmed what the detectives already knew, there was a code of silence in the streets, just like the police department, known as the blue wall of silence. They were now positive that someone knew more than they were willing to admit, at least to the police. That was usually the case in the black community, it crippled many police investigations. Black people were almost always distrustful of the police. They had little faith in the judicial system, partly because they bore the brunt of its one-sided justice. And to them, the system moved too slow and punishments weren't nearly harsh enough. On the other hand, street justice never disappointed them. The guilty parties were always dealt with swiftly and the punishment was always severe. The streets were the judge, jury and executioner.

"It's true, bad news sure does travel fast." Det. Scott thought to himself.

"Do you remember who told you that? Everything is off the record." Det. Scott asked.

"Yo, I ain't no snitch. You can put that on the record." Big Rock stated firmly.

Detectives Nilo and Scott didn't trust Big Rock at all. For someone who had such an intimate and personal relationship with Delilah, he didn't appear too sympathetic.

Though they couldn't put their finger on it, something just wasn't right with him or his story.

"So, you didn't catch the accident on the news?" Det. Nilo asked.

Big Rock wiped his face with his shaky hand. "Na man, I don't even watch TV, my ear is always to the streets. They gimme all the info I need. At first I didn't believe what happened to Delilah. I checked a few more sources, because I was hopin' it was a lie."

"What's up with your new album?" Det. Scott asked, pretending to be curious.

"It's on fire! It's definitely gonna go triple platinum." Big Rock answered. "It drops in December. Matter fact, Delilah, God bless her soul, is on two of the tracks."

Det. Nilo leaned in closer to Big Rock. "Now, let me get this straight, you and Delilah were seeing each other for about a year, correct?"

Big Rock shook his head. "Right. And?"

Det. Nilo nodded. "And you were also the executive producer of her debut album. You controlled her recording budgets, production and all the other stuff, right?"

Big Rock nodded. "Yeah. And? What's ya point?"

Scott stood from his seat. "Now, from what I understand, you and her ex-boyfriend, a known drug-dealer by the name of KB, didn't see eye to eye. Word is ya'll had some kind beef or something?"

Big Rock also stood. "I didn't have no beef wit him, I've never seen him a day in my life. He's in jail and I'm on the outside, what can he possibly do to me? He's no threat to me. It's not like he can get at me. Feel me? Delilah chose me, he should've left it at that. He just runnin' his mouf in jail."

Nilo looked confused. "And he should have respected the game right?"

Big Rock sighed in frustration. "I mean he should've recognized that he was cut the fuck off, he was out and I was in. But he kept playin' hisself, sweatin' her, callin' her, harassing her, threatening to kill her, all that bullshit."

Det. Nilo wrinkled his forehead. "Did you ever hear him threaten to kill her?"

"I seen the letters he wrote. He underlined all his threats in red ink." Big Rock's voice began to deepen. "Stevie Wonder coulda seen that!"

"Okay, calm down." Det. Nilo said sternly. "No need to get yourself all worked up. We'll get to the bottom of this."

Det. Scott pulled out a black pen and a small notebook. He began to take notes. "So after ya'll broke up, were you and Delilah still on good terms, or were ya'll no longer speaking?

Big Rock hung his head. His platinum jewelry made a loud swishing sound every time he moved.

"Na, I still had mad love for her." Big Rock said reluctantly. "We had a fallout cuz I found out about some foul shit she did in her past, and she lied to me about it. After

I got over that, it was all gravy."

Det. Nilo voice grew louder. "Like what? What did

she allegedly do?"

Big Rock scowled. "That's real personal fam! I don't

want to talk about it. I don't wanna put her business out in

the streets. She's dead, let her rest in peace. No need to go

into any of that."

Suddenly Det. Scott's pen stopped. "This is a murder

investigation, son. Nothing is personal!"

Big Rock glared at the two detectives. "Yo, why you

fuckin' yellin' at me? I didn't kill the girl!"

Det. Nilo pointed his finger at the nervous rap artist.

"Getting defensive? Huh?"

Det. Scott placed his hand on his partner's shoulder

and said. "Son, I understand that you are hurt and angry. No

one's accusing you of anything. If you loved her so much,

then you should want to help us find out who did this to her. Who killed Delilah Brown?"

Big Rock stared at the floor for a few seconds then look at Det. Scott and said. "Aaiight, my bad. She told me that she fucked that punk, Tito Diez. That Bitch-ass nigga!"

Det. Nilo smacked himself in the face sarcastically. "No shit? You sure?"

"Are you saying she fucked him while you two were together?" Det. Scott asked.

"You muthafuckin' right I'm sure! Got it right from the horses mouf!" Big Rock answered. "Na, they wasn't fuckin' while she was seein' me. It was a lil' before, but it still don't matter. If he's gonna be an executive, be a executive. He always tryin' to sleep with his female artists. He be stressin' them, put 'em under pressure."

Det. Nilo asked. "He's done this before? To Who? When? How many times?"

Big Rock nodded. "Hell yeah! Who ain't he done it to, that's the question. He did it lots of times, take my word on it! He's slimy like that!"

Det. Scott began to scribble furiously. "How was their relationship before and after the sex episode? Delilah and Tito's. Because you and Delilah's love affair was in the papers and on the TV every day, ya faces were plastered everywhere."

Big Rock cleared his throat nervously. "He hated that shit too. He hated her for siding wit me over him. If you ask me, it was definitely an ego thing. Her siding with me, that hurt his fuckin' pride."

"Well I'll be damned." Det. Nilo sighed. "Our boy Tito's a real piece of shit."

Det. Scott changed the subject abruptly. "Now, tell us about the shootout. What really went down? Who did what to whom?"

Big Rock's eyes grew wide in terror. "My lawyer said I can't talk about that."

Det. Scott repeated again in a tougher tone. "I said tell us about the damn shootout rapper boy. We're not asking you, we're telling you!"

Big Rock's face began to tremble with rage. "I was found not guilty at trial, by a jury of my peers. That's all I'm gonna say bout that. I could still be indicted by the Feds on weapons charges any fuckin' day now. Ya'll know how they play dirty. Next thing I know, the government'll subpoena you, so I won't talk about it no more. I ain't try'na tell on myself!"

Det. Nilo interrupted. "Do you think that shootout could have had anything to do with Delilah's murder? Maybe somebody wanted to even the score? She had any enemies you know of in the music industry?"

Big Rock angrily yelled. "How the fuck I'm suppose to know! I already told ya'll I was found not guilty! Are ya'll fuckin' listenin'? You want any more info on that, then read the damn trial transcripts. I ain't sayin no more bout it!"

Det. Nilo got in Big Rock's face, grabbed his collar and shoved him in anger. He said. "Let me tell you something, you and I both know you were guilty, you beat that case on a technicality. You've got that fancy, high-priced lawyer to thank for getting your ass off the hook. I don't care what you say, you are still a criminal in my book. You're a coward, you shot an unarmed woman in the face, you piece of crap, rap-crap!"

Det. Scott grabbed his partner. "I'm very sorry about that son. My partner takes things a little too personal sometimes. This is a very emotional case for him. He has a teenage daughter, you know."

Big Rock straightened up his clothing and fixed his chain. "I hear ya, but I ain't really feelin' ya partner all up in my grill like that. You know what, I'm through talking, arrest me or sumthin'. If ya'll ain't doin' that, ya'll gotta get out now! This lil Q&A session is over!" He shouted.

"Okay." Det. Nilo said, as he handed Big Rock his card. "We'll show ourselves out, but you keep ya eyes and ears open and give me a call if you hear or see anything that might interest us. Okay, Rocky?"

Big Rock grabbed his card and shoved it in his shirt pocket. He turned to the window and stared out aimlessly. His face was melancholy and filled with pain. It was as if the detectives had stirred up a well of intense emotions, or maybe it just actually hit him that Delilah was dead. He gritted his teeth, trying to contain the feelings.

"Yeah, aiiight! I'll do that." He said to the detectives.

Det. Nilo whispered to his partner as they exited the studio. "Now let's go and check out this KB guy. He might just be the missing link to solving this case."

"Yeah, that sounds like a plan. Then next we'll pay the shooting victim, Sandra Bullion, a visit. After that, we'll revisit Mr. Playboy, Tito Diez. I'm real anxious to speak with him again."

"Sounds like a plan to me partner." Det. Scott concurred.

"I knew you'd agree with me partner. You're a man after my own heart." Det. Nilo joked.

The two detectives felt they had some really good leads, something that was almost concrete. It would only be a matter of time before they cracked this case wide open. They felt for sure that their luck was about to change.

After the two detectives left, Big Rock needed a drink, bad. He went to the bar and poured himself a tall glass of Hennessey, wondering how much did they really know? He could tell they were holding back something and he prayed they couldn't tell what it was he was holding back His thoughts turned to the shooting incident outside of the Club that the detectives referred to. He couldn't bring himself to telling them the truth about the incident and how it

all went down. It all started with KB.

Chapter 5

KB had brought Delilah to him in the first place. The moment he saw her, he was open to her style. He knew she was KB's girl, and he knew KB well enough to know not to approach her. KB's name rang a bell all over the Bronx and Harlem and he definitely wasn't the man to cross. So Rock kept his distance and tried to keep everything professional. Then KB caught a Fed beef and got locked up. At first, Rock didn't know how long KB would be locked up, but when Delilah told him 15 years, he knew this was his chance to get with shorty. He knew Delilah still had feelings for KB, but he was Big Rock, the platinum artist and KB, gangster or no

gangster, was now just another faceless number in the

Federal prison system. He began taking Delilah everywhere

with him, sporting her so the world could see them together

and draw their own conclusions. He knew word would get

back to KB, but what could he do, locked up for 15 years?

Sure KB had guns on the street, but if Delilah chose him,

what was the beef? That's when Delilah told Rock that KB

was threatening her and how abusive he really was to her. He

became her shoulder to cry on, and then one day, he received

a call.

"Yo Rock, this is K. What the deal?" The voice

barked over the phone.

Rock knew exactly who it was, but what threw him

off was KB was supposed to be locked up, but didn't call

collect. "What up, KB? Where you at, dog?" Rock asked.

"You know where the fuck I'm at, you bitch ass nigga, or you wouldn't be runnin' around wit my bitch!" KB said, fuming.

"Ay yo KB, you ain't gotta." Rock began, but KB abruptly cut him off.

"Don't worry nigga, we ain't bout to beef over no pussy, but we will beef over my paper!" KB yelled.

"Your paper? What paper?" Rock replied, unsure what KB was talking about.

"The paper you owe me for bringing you that trifling bitch in the first place! My peoples comin' to see you and I want 50 cent up front and a dime off every album she sold, you hear me?"

Rock couldn't believe his ears, true KB was gangster, but surely he didn't think he could extort him from prison! Rock chuckled. "50 cents, you mean 50 grand? Yo son, I don't owe you a fuckin' dime. Yeah true, you hooked me up,

but ahhh, you need to talk to Delilah about any paper comin'
to you."

"Oh, so you think it's a game? Nigga, I brought that
bitch to you and believe me, I can take her away!" KB said,
pissed off because Rock was playing him just because he
was locked up.

"Whatever, dog. Do what you gotta do." Rock said,
then hung up the phone.

Talking to KB, Rock tried to sound tough, but
immediately after the call, he beefed up his security tenfold.
He knew never to underestimate KB, even with him being
locked up. He never told Delilah about the call.

Rock sipped his Henny and thought about Delilah
and how sorry he was that she got caught up in all this. Rock
didn't consider himself a snitch, but before the cops found
out how he was connected in all this, he'd tell them what he
knew. KB killed Delilah.

Ms. Brown glanced at the clock. It was already 6 p.m. She couldn't believe how the hours had flown by. The couple of days since the accident felt like seconds. The hunger in her stomach now weakened her. Dizziness began to set in. She knew that with her diabetic condition she had to eat something soon. She decided to turn the page and read a little bit more before getting something to eat.

February 28th

Hey ya'll. What's good. Sorry I took so long to write again. It's been so hectic. I performed at the all-star game last week. It was off the chain! People were goin' outta their minds, showing me love. Everyone was singing my songs! Can you believe it? I felt like I had the flu, but I decided to do it anyway. I felt kinda spacey when I got off stage. All the cute basketball players were sweatin' me. But, you know I know what they about, celebrity ass and one-night stands. I was kickin' it wit this one guy, Rick Jonathan. He plays point guard for the New York Knicks. A real cutey! He knows

Alamo, who works promotions for the label. But anyway, I wouldn't play Big Rock like that, even though things ain't all that good between us. I'm still not that slimy type of chick who fucks around on her man.

So anyway, I went to the doctor yesterday. He said I didn't have the flu, it was simply exhaustion. I've been pushing myself too hard lately. He suggested that I take about month off, kick back and take it easy. You know, I'm like, whatever. You only live once, so I'm goin' to ride the wave while I'm hot. While I still got the damn chance! Jenny is saying that I should listen to the doctor, but I gotta do me, you know. I gotta do another video next week. The doctor also said that I may be drinking too much alcohol and not enough water. I never used to drink that much alcohol until after what happened with me and Tito. I've just been partying a lot and having a good time. Jenny says I know gotta slow down though, but I still feel like I gotta live it up.

This radio station DJ was interviewing me the other day, she asked me about some old police report my mom filed when I was a kid. She said my dad molested me. I don't know where they dig this shit up from. I started crying and ran out of the station. My publicist was so pissed, she canceled the interview. I called my grandma to make sure she didn't hear it. Honestly, I don't remember what happened between me and my dad. I remember he used to take me to the park and buy me hot dogs and pretzels, that's all I remember. Wait a minute, I do remember havin' to go to a therapist, her name was Miss Thomas. I went to see her for years, but when I turned sixteen, my grandma said I didn't have to go anymore. We just talked about life and how I felt. She was a cool-ass white lady. I told her over and over that I didn't remember nothin' that happened between me and my dad, I was too young. My dad's name was Arnold. Come to think of it, I don't really remember my mom either. My grandma tells me she was beautiful. She always joked that I got my big butt from her. Grandma said that she used to have to beat the men off my mom with a bat. My dad got her involved in drugs, the wild nightlife, I guess. I don't know the whole story, but somehow she ended up dead. My grandmother always seemed to think that Arnold had everything to do with her death. I can only go by her word, I don't know anything else but that. But anyway, it doesn't really bother me, because I never really knew either of them. I was raised by my grandma. My grandpa died from lung cancer when I was two.

But all this talk of this police report, I don't know. Who would let such a thing out like that? Tito called me and told me that I better not make any comments about it. He is such a mean, cold person. He treats me like I'm his child now, but he didn't act like that before he got what he wanted. I just don't understand men sometimes. Why do they always see women as an object to be conquered and destroyed. Sometimes I feel like they see us as a toy they use to finish the job of sexually pleasing themselves. What about our feelings? When they are done with us, they just toss you out in the trash like an old rag. I don't understand that. Sometimes I ask, why even bother? Sometimes I hate men so much. They can't get past thinking 'bout themselves. Sometimes I think Big Rock ain't no different. I've never caught him, but I think he might be doing some things behind my back. He has this one dancer who is always looking at me sideways. I don't trust it, but we'll see. One way or another, what you do in the dark, always comes out in the light. Well, I gotta get some rest. C- ya. -D-Nice!

In dismay, Ms. Brown shook her head. Her only grandchild's life was taken. The kid was only beginning to learn the painful lessons that life had to teach her. She was so intelligent, but she was just a kid. Delilah had already been through so much. Ms. Brown would give anything just to hug her, to hold her one more time. She felt a little guilty. Had she not given the child enough guidance? Had she failed in raising her granddaughter correctly? Delilah was having inappropriate relationships with men, drinking, partying and living fast. What went wrong? Melinda's eyes filled with tears. She decided she had to get up and fix herself something to eat before she passed out again. "God please give me strength" She whispered.

The green, four door Ford Taurus left a trail of dust, as the two New York City homicide detectives drove up the winding unpaved prison road. It had been a long flight from New York to Texas, and this rental was a piece of crap. Dets. Scott and Nilo had finally secured the documents they needed to question an out of state federal prisoner. They stopped briefly at a gas station for directions, then pulled up to the Federal Correctional Institution in Texarkana, Texas. They were physically drained from the long trip, yet mentally sharp from the thought of breaking open this mysterious homicide.

The prison was old and gloomy looking. To these detectives, it bore a slight resemblance to a medieval castle. There were rows upon rows of sharp angry looking barbed wire, as far as the eye could see, surrounding a menacing fifteen foot fence, with an armed guard that stood watch. The dreary guard tower that overlooked its perimeter was the last line of defense that society had from the convicts. The entire atmosphere looked depressing from the outside. The detectives could only imagine what horrors lay inside the prison. Just the mere thought of being confined there, sent chills down the detectives' spines.

KB had been sentenced to fourteen years in the Federal system, this was just one of his many stops in the years to come. KB and an associate had sold numerous guns to an undercover federal agent over a six-month time span. During the course of their trial, his co-defendant cut a deal and agreed to testify against him, in exchange for a lighter sentence. His co-defendant successfully pointed the finger at

KB as the mastermind behind the illegal purchase of the guns down south. He claimed KB ordered him to buy semi-automatic pistols and to scratch off the identification numbers. That testimony sealed KB's fate, and right in the middle of the trial, he took a plea bargain.

Even though KB was a known gangster all across New York City, he had never been convicted of a crime before. The government slapped him with a fourteen-year sentence for his first offense. This was an all too common story for young minorities in America, they were playing a game that they couldn't win. Most never even knew what they were up against until incarcerated and faced with the heavy legal ramifications of their illegal acts.

The detectives moved in slow motion as they approached the federal facility. The case was barely a week old and here they were out of state chasing leads. There was never a dull moment in this line of work. They had received many leads and a lot of information, but still there was no definite suspect. KB was a very important link in the chain of this murderous drama.

The two detectives marched up a flight of stairs into the prison, unsure of what to expect. This could either be the answer to their prayers or just another wild goose chase. They were struggling to stay optimistic, but admittedly, they were beginning to feel a little discouraged. So many people were telling lies to cover up personal issues. It seemed that no one, except Ms. Brown, truly cared about Delilah. Everyone else just seemed to have jumped on her bandwagon and then jumped right off after she died.

Det. Scott remembered the awesome pain that his family went through when his daughter passed away. In Delilah's situation, there didn't seem to be the same remorse. No one, other than her grandmother, seemed to be truly grieving over her death. In Det. Scott's eyes, this made everyone a potential suspect. They all seemed to have a hidden agenda, a motive for murder.

"Right this way guys, we've been expecting you." A uniformed correctional officer said as he led the detectives into a small visiting room.

The detectives followed without saying a word, although they secretly despised this country bumpkin. Just like country folk dislike city slickers, these city slickers despised country folks.

The room they entered was completely empty except for two correctional officers standing guard at the door. One of the officers said. "This room is reserved just for you guys and your suspect. Have fun, don't do nothing I wouldn't do. Inmates have a tendency to slip and fall and bump their heads in this room, if ya know what I mean."

The young officer's face lit up with pride. He seemed happy to be aiding in a real law enforcement investigation. He was tired of being perceived as a rent-a-cop or a fake policeman. This was actually a little exciting for him.

"Thanks for the tip. We'll take it into consideration."
Det. Scott said, as the guard pulled their seats out for them.

"No problem." The guard said. "If you boys need any
assistance, just holler and old Jimbo will come runnin'. My
dad was a Texarkana Sheriff on the Arkansas side, so I know
what you boys are up against everyday."

"You don't say." Det. Scott faked interest.

"Yes sir. Fifteen years, famous for breaking up the
biggest cow tipping ring this side of Texas."

"Wow!" Det. Nilo exclaimed. "I think I heard of ya
old man."

The officer smiled brightly. "You probably have.
Now let me hush up. I'll get your man in here now."

"He's a real piece work huh?" Det. Nilo quirked,
after the man shut the door.

"Well, you know the federal government will hire
anyone. They're all probably related up here. You don't have

to be a rocket scientist to get a job in corrections." Det. Scott answered.

"Ain't that the truth!" Nilo said, and both men chuckled like sixth graders in a school lunchroom. "He sure is dumb as a brick, it must run in the family."

After a few minutes, a tall, well-built, young black man entered the room, followed by two officers. He wore institution issued brown khakis and a pair of shiny black boots. His chiseled face was groomed impeccably. He had a small white nametag stitched to his khaki shirt with his name and inmate number, K. Banks, 0-99999-089.

The two detectives stood up as the young man entered the room.

Recognition flashed across both KB's and Scott's faces simultaneously. The meeting made KB smile and Scott curse under his breath. Nilo didn't miss a beat.

"So you're a detective now, huh?" KB cracked.

"And you're still a criminal." Scott replied dryly.

"Some things never change, do they?" KB smiled as he took a seat at the table. "So I guess the Bronx is all safe and secure knowing Officer Scott is on the job."

"And the infamous KB is behind bars." Det. Scott shot back.

Unable to understand what was passing between the two men, Det. Nilo cut in. "I'm Detective Nilo, NYPD." Nilo informed him, as the two guards exited the room.

"And that's supposed to mean what to a nigga in Texas?" KB quipped.

Nilo hated a wise ass. "Look son." He replied. "The flight was coach, it's 104 in the shade and the food in Texas sucks. So, I'm really not in the mood. You know why we're here and you know what we wanna know, so start talking."

"First of all, I don't see no lawyer in this room." KB laughed, trying to get in a comfortable position, despite the handcuffs and full body restraints. "Second, I don't know anything about nothing no how."

"Try Delilah Brown. Name ring a bell?" Det. Nilo asked.

KB tried desperately to hold his composure. "What about her?

"So you mean to tell me you don't know she's dead, or rather, that she was murdered?" Det. Nilo wanted to know.

Det. Scott interjected. "Mr. Banks, I'm real sorry about your current living conditions, I couldn't imagine being in your situation. But a man creates his own conditions. You made your bed, so now you gotta lie in it. I'm sure it is rougher than I could ever imagine. But put a 'S' on your chest and handle it. Listen, I don't want to waste your time or ours. You know why we're here, Delilah's dead. What do you know? Let's make this quick."

KB lowered his head sadly. "I was kinda hoping you guys had some information to give me about that. I don't know nuthin' but what I read in the papers and magazines, and you know how that go. Every other newspaper has a different story. I'm confused, I don't know what to believe."

Det. Nilo stood in anger. "You don't know nuthin' huh!" He screamed. "You sent the girl twenty psychotic letters, Jenny Santiago filed a police report a year and a half ago, Delilah was afraid! You threatened to kill her over fifty times, you little jealous hearted prick! Now you don't know nuthin'?"

KB stood to his feet. "Let me tell you somethin' right now, you fake Dirty Harry ass muthafucka. In case you haven't checked, I ain't goin' nowhere! I can't kill someone in New York City from Texarkana, Texas, you idiot! That's physically impossible."

One of the guards stuck his head in the door. "Everything okay in here detectives? Do you need help?"

"No, we're just fine. Everything is under control. Thanks." Det. Scott answered.

The guard stared sternly at KB. "Banks, you ain't givin' these guys any problems, are you? Cuz you know what we do to rebels around here? Don't you?"

KB glared at the guard. He hated how they tried to talk to him like a child. He was a grown ass man. He wished he could choke the life out of this correctional officer. "Mind ya business! Can't you see this is a confidential visit?" He answered defiantly.

"Okay, Banks keep runnin' your big mouth. I already done told you one day it's gonna get you in a world of trouble." The guard said with a sly smirk. "Just remember, when they leave, we still gonna be here brother!"

KB sighed and ignored the guard. "What do you want from me?" He asked Det. Scott. KB's frustration and anger were visible in his face. "Yes, she was my girl, I loved her. Yes, she pissed me off by runnin' around town with that fake gangster rapper, Big Rock's gay ass. Delilah wasn't always like that. She changed. Fame went to her head."

Det. Scott looked intrigued. "Well, we have information that links you to several drug related murders. We have reason to believe that you may have ordered the hits from here. I'm sure the F.B.I. has also questioned you, correct?"

KB rolled his eyes. "Whatever. I don't know nuttin' bout that. They ain't got nothin' and neither do you."

Det. Nilo snarled. "It's only a matter of time dirt bag!"

Det. Scott's eyes shut his partner's mouth immediately. He turned to KB. "Look, I'm not investigating anything but Delilah's murder. That's my job, to bring the killer to justice for her grandmother. Obviously, this was a set up, the car accident was to cover up the bullet in her head." He said.

"What would that have to do with me?" KB barked. "I was in jail when it happened. Unless you got informants

spying on me, or a sworn affidavit, then that shit you talkin'
is hearsay. Aiight!"

"Hearsay my ass!" Det. Nilo yelled. Det. Scott's
glance silenced him once again.

"Look." Det. Scott said, after a dirty look directed at
his partner, "We have reason to believe the shootout last year
was between Big Rock and Johnny Blaze. We know that
Pinky Blades used to push major weight for you in Harlem,
right?"

KB shook his head. "Never heard of no fuckin' Pinky
Blades. Who the fuck is that clown? I do my dirt by my
lonely. Matter fact, I ain't saying nothin', end of
conversation. It's a wrap fellas."

Det. Scott nodded. "Okay, but just tell me something.
Why did you order the hit on Big Rock that night and try to
make it look like a regular club beef turned deadly?"

KB laughed hard. "You fuckin' cops give me way too
much credit. Ya'll think I'm fuckin' God or sumthin' on the

streets. Like I can just snap my fingers and muthafucka get

killed. I had nuttin', I repeat nuttin', to do with any of that.

You watch too much cable."

Det. Nilo flinched as if he was going for another

outburst. He bit his lip and remained quiet.

Scott chuckled. "Okay, okay. Well KB, we flew all

the way down here for nothing. Tell us something, anything.

Amuse us. Do it for Delilah, if you really loved her as you

say you did."

KB stared at the ground for a few seconds. The

young convict took in a long deep breath. He peered across

the table at the two detectives with a look of pure disdain.

"Let me say one thing." He said calmly. "After this, being

that I am a suspect in a murder, I ain't saying nothin' else

without a lawyer present."

"What is it KB?" Det. Scott leaned in closer.

KB eyed the ceiling for a moment, then continued.

"See, there is one thing you gotta remember. Nowadays

things are so twisted. Times have changed. Your best rappers are suburban white boys, your best golf and tennis players are black people. See, nowadays all the gangsters wanna be rappers and all the rappers wanna be gangsters."

"What in the world does that mean?" Det. Nilo blurted.

"That's it." KB answered. "I ain't got no more rap, the party's over." He rose from his seat.

Scott scribbled the convict's words on his notepad. "Fair enough." He said. "But, I'm sure you'll see us again before it's over."

"I hope so." KB responded, in defiance, "You pigs are the only visits I get."

"Get back to your playhouse punk!" Det. Nilo kicked his chair under the table violently. He couldn't believe he flew way into the middle of nowhere for this nonsense. He knew he shouldn't have listened to Scott, but that was Det. Scott. He was Mr. Cool, Mr. Know it all. "What a waste of time." Det. Nilo complained. "But you got plenty to of time waste."

Det. Scott tapped his finger on the table as KB was escorted back to his cell. "Maybe not." He said. "Maybe not."

As they drove away from the prison, Nilo turned to Scott and asked. "So, what's the story with Banks back there? You two got some sort of history?"

Scott drove on silently, then replied. "Just a young punk that I knew from my beat days, nothing major."

"What do you think of his story? Think he really did order that hit on Brown from the joint?"

Scott shrugged. "He definitely has the means. My sources say KB is still a major player in the Bronx and Harlem. And he surely had a motive. He seems bitter about how things went with Delilah. Some guys can't handle rejection." He explained, but Nilo got the feeling that Scott wasn't only talking about KB.

"Tell me something, Scott. What makes you get up every morning, take a shit and then spend your day risking your life in a losing battle out in the streets?"

Scott glanced over at Nilo and smirked. "It's a dirty job, but somebody's gotta do it." And with that, they returned to their usual silence."

Chapter 6

"You have a collect call from KB, will you accept? Press nine if you will accept."

Sasha quickly pressed nine and turned the TV down.

"Sasha."

"Hey, baby! How you doin'? Did you get the pictures I sent you? I still look good in a thong, don't I Boo?" Sasha flirted.

The thought of the pictures made KB hard just thinking about them, but he had more pressing business to address. "Yeah ma, they were straight. But yo, did you get my letter?"

"I got it. Were you serious about all that?"

"Look yo, I told you from jump that if you gonna be with me then be wit me. Period. Don't ever question me. Either you is or you ain't wit me." KB stated firmly, wondering why he even fucked with Sasha in the first place.

"I'm wit you, baby. You can count on me." She assured him.

"Cool. That's what I wanna hear. You see, B?" KB asked, not wanting to say Pinkie Blades' name over the phone.

"Yeah I saw him. He said you know he got you."

"Well look, some shit just jumped off so we gonna have to step it up, aiight. I just got a visit from an old friend." KB told her.

"Who?"

"Fuckin' Scott!"

"Scott? Scott? Scott?" Sasha repeated, wondering what he had to with all this.

"Yeah, Scott. Crooked ass Bronx Scott and he is a detective on Delilah's case."

Sasha was silent.

"Sasha, you still there?"

"Yeah Boo, I'm here. What's Scott...."

KB cut her off. "I don't know. Just do like I said in the letter and keep your eyes open, aiight?"

"Always."

"Okay, I gotta go."

"Boo, I love you." Sasha purred.

KB hung up with a chuckle.

Love? Who really believed in that anymore. Especially to a nigga in the joint wit over a decade of time to do behind iron and concrete. And coming from Sasha, it was really a joke, because he already knew she was fucking with some kid out of Co-op City. Oh well, as long as she played her position, KB thought. After that she'll be useless anyway.

As KB walked back to his cell, he contemplated how round the world truly is. The same Scott that used to provide his drug operation protection and had even killed niggas for money, was now investigating the same kind of murder he had carried out in the past. In a world like this, it's hard to tell the cops from the robbers sometimes. But KB knew one thing, whatever Scott knew or thought he knew, KB would bet his partner Nilo would never know the whole story.

Ms. Brown juggled her keys nervously before finding the right one. It was hard to believe that she had just come home from her granddaughter's funeral. It was almost harder to believe that almost a week had flew by since the fatal accident. The old grandmother thought that identifying Delilah's charred corpse was the most difficult thing she would ever have to do, she was wrong. Standing at that funeral, watching them lower her granddaughter's coffin into the ground was the absolute worst moment of her life. She always assumed Delilah would be the one to bury her.

The funeral procession seemed to stretch for miles. Expensive foreign cars drove almost bumper to bumper, making up the core of the procession. Celebrities from all fields of entertainment imaginable, hopped out of the fleets of black limos that stretched for miles. They came from far and wide, representing the four corners of the world, gathered to pay their last respects to one of their own. The burial ceremony was elaborate, fit for a queen or some high-ranking foreign dignitary.

For Delilah's final farewell, no expense was spared. For those who weren't fortunate enough to be a part of the funeral procession or witness it up close, they gathered outside, hoping for a small glimpse.

Hundreds of well-wishers, reporters and fans who weren't able to attend the private funeral, lined the streets that led to the cemetery. They were hoping to catch a glimpse of Delilah's casket or someone famous attending the funeral. They sang Delilah's hit records, turning a somber mood into a joyous occasion.

Delilah's casket was a work of art in itself, a marble masterpiece. It carried her remains to her final resting place in the same elegance that she was accustomed to. The scent of fresh flowers filled the church. As Melinda looked at the young girls who attended the funeral, she couldn't help but remember her daughter, Felicia. This deja vu was devastating.

The happy mood at the ceremony was just like Delilah would have wanted it. Delilah would have asked that people rejoice and be glad. There were some people, including Melinda, who weren't so festive. A few people were breaking down, screaming and fainting. There were so many folks that Melinda had never seen before, just going to pieces as the casket was lowered into the ground. As the children's choir softly sang "Ave Maria", Melinda's heart broke. The small children were dressed in all white, swaying gently from side to side as they sang. It all seemed so unreal. It was like a beautiful dream, but at the same time, a nightmare.

People from all walks of life and all ages, even the Mayor of New York, stood up and told stories about their experiences with Delilah. Everyone had such wonderful memories of her granddaughter. Melinda was so proud of the great friendships and bonds that Delilah had formed in such a short time. People absolutely loved her and it showed. Her stylist said. "She was as real as they came. If she said she was going to do it, she did it. If she was down with you, she was down with you until the end."

The finality of her granddaughter's death suddenly hit Melinda like a sledgehammer. Tears poured down her cheeks uncontrollably. She was like a big baby, as sobs racked her frail frame. "The Lord giveth and the good Lord taketh away." She thought. Now she was alone in this cold, cruel world. Away from all the well-wishers, she sat in her favorite chair in her humble home. Thoughts of her deceased granddaughter flourished through her mind. It was strange knowing she'd never walk through her door again. There would be no late night bi-coastal phone calls, checking to see if she was okay. The cold reality was she was dead, gone before her time.

"I love you Delilah." She whispered. Ms. Brown was grateful to the church for handling the funeral arrangements and the transportation and all. Mr. Diez was most gracious in agreeing to foot the bill. So many people had love for Delilah. It was a blessing to see how many people she had touched.

Glancing at her wristwatch, Ms. Brown noticed it was five 5:30 p.m. Minister Jacobs said that he would stop over at about six or so. She scratched her itchy scalp, believing she was forgetting something. Her memory was fading fast. After pacing back and forth across the floor, it suddenly hit her. "The book!" She remembered all of a sudden. I have to finish reading it, I owe Delilah that much. She would want me to find out what happened.

"Now where did I put that book?" She thought, aloud. Pausing for a moment, she summoned every working brain cell to help her remember. Trying as she might, she couldn't recall its location no matter how hard she concentrated. In frustration, she fell back onto the couch. "Oww! This pillow is pretty hard." Melinda said aloud. She reached under the pillow and discovered it was the book. Luckily, she had taken her bookmark from her Bible and used it to remember where she had left off. She opened Delilah's book and began to read, hoping to finish a few more pages before the pastor arrived for some one on one counseling.

September 7th

Hey young world. It's me, ya girl, Delilah! It's been a minute since I wrote, but I've just been so busy. It's been crazy. I've been in the studio all day and all night. I've been

working like a dog, trying to finish my next project. Gotta

ride the wave. I feel so tired sometimes. The doctor keeps

telling me that I am stressed out and need a break. I'm not

trying to hear it. I can't right now, gotta get mine while I'm

hot. Me and Big Rock have been doing fine since the trial

ended. Oh, let me tell ya what happened. See, Big Rock loves

to party. He loves to be seen in all of the hot spots around

town. I think he clubs a little too much. Too much of one

thing isn't good for anyone. You know me, I don't mind, I

didn't say nuttin'. He's a grown man. Anyway, me and him

were Fred Astair and Ginger Rogers or James Dean and

Marilyn Monroe. Everywhere we went, someone was always

snapping pictures. Every move we make together is a media

story. Sometimes I feel like he is just using me as a trophy to

make himself look good, you know a career boost. I had so

much fun with him though. It made me feel like a princess,

special, ya know? I was his and he was mine. All for one and one for all. Things at home weren't always perfect, but when

we stepped out, we looked like everything was perfect.

But anyway, it was New Year's Eve and we were

leaving Club Cheetah in Manhattan. Big Rock was drunk as

ever. He kept trying to get me to drink too, but I was just

chillin'. It was getting late and I was hungry, so I started

nagging Rock because I was ready to leave. As we were

leaving, he started throwing money into the crowd like he

was ballin' out of control. He had like twenty grand on him

in hundred dollar bills. We only had three bodyguards that

night and things were getting wild. Some guy in the crowd,

and I swear I think I had seen him somewhere before, he

threw the money back in Big Rock's face! Like yeah nigga.

He said something about not needing no corny rapper's

money. I remember feeling like something was about to pop

off. Then all of the sudden I heard gun shots, bitches is

screamin', niggas is hittin' the floor. Everything happened so fast. In a few seconds, we were running for our lives. We jumped into our limo and sped off.

A couple of blocks away, the cops pulled us over and they told us that a woman got shot in the face at the club. Big Rock had a gat under the seat, but I was right next to him inside the club, I knew that he didn't shoot nobody. They told Rock that they dragged one of his peoples, Lil Smooth, outside of the club, he had a gat on him, it was in his waistband. Anyway, they let me go and Big Rock and Lil Smooth got locked up. After that incident, everyone kept telling me to leave Big Rock alone. Everybody told me that he would be heading upstate for a charge that serious, but I decided to stick by him through the whole trial. Why would I leave him? I'm not like that, I stand by my man. I know how shit go, when you get out of the streets, haters wanna pull you back. The whole situation was just plain stupid. I can't even believe it happened, and it happened so fast. I'm glad nobody got killed. It's messed up though. Lil Smooth got convicted and Big Rock was found not guilty. Since then, he has been a changed man. He ain't into playin' Big Willie no more. Now he has a low profile. He watches where he go and who he be wit. The trial took a lot outta him, his life was on the line. The stress took a toll on him and it cost him a lot of paper to beat the charges.

I've been having some trouble getting paid from the record label. Jenny told me not to worry, she's on top of it. She has been such a blessing to me through all of this, She's been closer to me than a sister. I really don't know what I'd do without that crazy girl. It still makes me a little sad that Sasha won't speak to us anymore. We were all so close. We did everything together. We were thicker than thieves, but that was then and this is now. Things definitely have changed. But anyway, my grandmother said it's natural for women to not get along with each other. So I guess I'll just live with it.

Oh, I almost forgot. It's probably nothing, but it was kind of weird, ya know. Anyway, there's this guy, I don't know how he knows, but everywhere I am, he's there. I pointed him out to Jenny and she said she would keep her eyes open. I've had plenty of stalkers that send me crazy stuff. One even sent me a wedding ring, an expensive one, too! Of course, I didn't send it back, but anyway, back to this guy. You see, I've met him before at one of my shows or something. I think he's a security guard or some type of military cat because he's real stiff like, ya know? When we met, he didn't act all crazy or nothing, it was just the way he looked at me that gave me the chills. He told me how much he loved my music and he wished me the best, then he left. After that, wherever I go, I usually see him looking at me, watching me with that same look. It's crazy. I hope he's not dangerous. He doesn't seem to be, but the world is a crazy place, so you never know. Like I said, hopefully it's nothing but I just wanted ya'll to know that the love stuff I get, ain't

always all good. Fame is crazy! One...Dee

Chapter 7

Detectives Nilo and Scott fidgeted anxiously in Mr.

Diez's office. It was the day after Delilah's funeral, and it

had been over a week since their last visit. Nilo always hated

the way people who felt they were important liked to make

people wait. Nilo's mind was in over drive. He read the court

transcripts of Big Rock's trial. He had also poured through

Delilah's financial records and royalty statements, finding

some fuzzy math. KB's words still rang in his ear. It seemed

as if this beautiful young girl had been caught up in

something that was bigger than she was.

"Sorry gentlemen." Mr. Diez said smoothly, while stepping into the office. "Mondays are always hectic."

"I understand." Det. Scott sighed.

"Well then, what can I do for you today?" Diez asked, slicking his wet looking hair back.

"Well." Det. Scott smirked. "We felt the need to ask you a few more questions about Delilah and her financial standing and royalties."

Diez nodded calmly. "I'll be glad to help you with that. Let me buzz my accounting guy." Diez, in true chairman's fashion, buzzed the accountant's office on his phone. "Harry?"

The voice on the other end of the phone answered instantly. "Yeah boss?"

Diez ignored the greeting. "Can you come up here and have a talk with me and these two detectives about Delilah's statements?"

"Sure boss, I'll be right up."

Det. Nilo's teeth were grinding together. "Who did this guy think he was?" He thought to himself.

"He'll be right up." Diez said, strolling over to the bar. "Get you guys anything?"

Det. Nilo was not amused. "No thanks."

Diez poured himself a shot. "Well, I'm gonna have one. It's one of those days." Det. Nilo waited for Diez to take a quick sip of his drink. Then he blurted out his thoughts. "Diez, were you sleeping with the little girl?"

Det. Scott couldn't believe his ears. "Nilo!" He shouted.

Diez dropped his glass onto the hardwood floor and the pieces scattered everywhere. "That is none of your business! We're all grown here" He responded in a very low, but stern tone. "I didn't kill that girl!"

Det. Nilo stood up pointing a shaky finger at Diez. "You little pervert! How could you take advantage of a little girl? I oughta...."

Triple Crown Publications Presents   Diva

"Nilo!" Det. Scott grabbed his partner by the arm to shut him up.

The accountant entered the room and interrupted the tension. "How are you gents?" The white haired man said, as he shook the detectives hands. Det. Nilo and Diez's eyes remained locked on each other the whole time. Det. Scott felt terribly uncomfortable. He knew he wouldn't get anywhere with Diez now that he was on the defense. He decided he had to try to calm things down.

"So." Det. Scott started. "Mr. accountant money man, I understand that Delilah's first album made a gross profit of about twenty five million dollars, yet her statements show that she owed Intersound three million dollars at the time of her death. How is that?"

The accountant rifled through his paper work. "Well sir, and my name is Harry Yantsen, you've got to understand the music business accounting. It's unlike any other business. See, the million dollar videos, limo rides, stylists,

150

tours, producer fees, studio time, clothes, jewelry, it all amounts to a loan against her portion of the net profit, which is only fifteen percent to begin with."

Det. Scott was confused. "So you guys get to keep your eighty-five percent, and charge all of these millions to her percentage before she gets paid?"

The accountant smiled. "Basically."

Det. Nilo laughed. "Sounds like we're in the wrong business after all."

"Shut up Nilo." Det. Scott whispered. "So." He continued. "Delilah lived a life of luxury, but only on the loan, not on her own royalties that she earned, right?"

"Basically. The record company never fully recouped our expenditures against her percentage." The accountant said.

"So why was she complaining about having trouble getting her money?"

"Well, it looks like she had a five million dollar budget for her next album." The accountant answered.

"Another loan?" Det. Scott asked.

"Basically." The accountant said, rifling through his papers again.

"So who controlled these funds, how they were dispersed?"

Harry glanced at Diez and then answered. "Jenny Santiago, of course. That's the only person Delilah trusted, her right hand woman."

"Well." Det. Scott asked. "What about song writer's royalties and that kind of stuff? Who controlled those?"

Harry looked at Diez once again.

After a pause, Diez answered. "Big Rock. Big Rock controlled all of that stuff."

Det. Nilo's knee was shaking in frustration. He couldn't hold it any longer. "You loved her didn't you,

Tito?" Nilo's voice quivered in anger. "She was a child, you freak!"

Diez's head dropped in embarrassment. "I have nothing to say about that detective. Aren't we here to talk about royalties?"

"Sure." Det. Scott responded. He knew he would get more about their relationship later. "That's all for now." Det. Scott said softly. As the cunning detective stood from his seat, he casually posed a question to the record company chairman.

"Diez." He scratched his head nonchalantly. "Before we leave, answer me one question."

Diez stared at Det. Scott. "Anything, what is it?"

"Well." Det. Scott said. "I just wanted to know why Delilah was suing Intersound for three million dollars."

Diez's eyes grew red with anger. "We were settling amicably out of court before the accident detective."

"Is that so?"

"Yes. Would you like me to call business affairs to bring up the paperwork, detective?"

Det. Scott straightened his jacket and headed for the door. "That won't be necessary Tito. We'll be in touch."

Det. Nilo walked cockily behind his partner. "You better believe it." He quirked.

After a brief nap, Ms. Brown was awakened abruptly by the loud rapping at the door. She instantly knew that it had to be the pastor. Six o'clock on the dot. He was always punctual. She threw her old sweater over her shoulders and headed for the door. After straightening her clothes for a quick second, she let him in. "Pastor Jacobs!" She felt a breath of relief. She didn't want to be alone.

"Hi Sister Brown." The pastor smiled. Pastor Jacobs had been a solid rock for Ms. Brown for so long. The entire ordeal had been so taxing, so frustrating. The pastor had provided much needed spiritual love and guidance.

"Sister Brown." He said calmly. "I just wanted to come by after the funeral to make sure you were okay and that your faith is still strong."

Melinda sighed. She didn't want to disappoint Pastor Jacobs, but this was a rough one. She did in fact question God's purpose on this one. Why allow such a wonderful young girl to lose her life so unexpectedly? Why, after she had already suffered so much? She didn't deserve it. Why didn't she live to see her grandchildren? Why do serial killers get to die warm in their beds and not Delilah? The truth was, Ms. Brown was angry with God. She had served him faithfully for over fifty years. She prayed to him every morning and night. She volunteered at the church, she gave her all. The only thing she had left, the only person she loved unconditionally, was that little girl. Yes, she was angry. She didn't understand it. She decided not to say anything to Pastor Jacobs, but the feelings boiled inside of her whole body.

"Please." Pastor Jacobs seemed all knowing. "I understand your sorrow and anger. But you may be looking at things the wrong way Melinda."

"What do you mean Pastor?"

"Well, have you ever heard of the saying, that the glass is either half full or half empty?"

She nodded in agreement.

"Well." Pastor Jacobs continued. "God giveth and He taketh away. Your granddaughter was a blessing from the moment she came into this world, every second that you spent with her was a blessing, but it was never promised."

"I don't understand Pastor." Melinda sat down on the couch and began to rub her forehead. It was a serious workload to hold back her tears.

"Well Sister, God never promised us that we were guaranteed to live ten, twenty, eighty years. He told us to live day by day. He told us to love one another. He warned us that we would suffer on this earth, but in the end it glorifies him because he will pull us through. We just have to trust in him. We will not always understand. Just like when Delilah was a little girl and she touched the stove and you slapped her hand. She didn't understand at all, but in the end it was all for the good."

Ms. Brown tried to reply, but the tears began to cascade down her cheeks. The pain was unbearable. She sobbed. "But it's not fair. She was only eighteen years old Pastor!"

"Yes Sister. Some children do not live past a day. Those eighteen years were a blessing. All we can do is thank God for that and understand that He don't make mistakes. Allow yourself to grieve, feel the pain. Don't fight it, then He'll give you the strength to go on."

Ms. Brown buried her head in the Pastor's chest. "I can't go on." She cried. "It hurts so bad. It's impossible to live. I just can't. It's hard to eat, to sleep. Please Pastor."

Pastor Jacobs shed a quick tear. He hurried to wipe it before Melinda saw it. He knew that he had to be strong for this woman. He just held her, rocking her back and forth gently. Melinda's tears soaked his shirt.

"It's okay to cry." He whispered. Silently the pastor prayed that the good Lord would have mercy on this woman and give her peace.

Ms. Brown was so grateful that Pastor Jacobs came by. They spent hours talking, crying and praying together. That man was definitely a gift from God. The old woman was sad to see the Pastor leave, but it was already past ten p.m., and Lord knows she needed some rest. Her entire body ached. It was weird to think about the effects of mental anguish on the body. She slipped off her shoes and began to massage her sore old feet. This instantly reminded her of Delilah. Some nights, after a tour or a show, Delilah would come home and rub her grandma's feet. She was such a caring, sweet girl. Melinda wanted to cry but her eyes simply refused. There were no more tears left inside of her. It was like God wanted her to stop crying and be strong. As she lay back on the couch she hit her head on the edge of a book. The book, she had forgotten about it again! Goodness, she should have shown it to Pastor Jacobs.

Her weary hands opened it slowly. She found the exact spot where she left her bookmark. She always kept her glasses on a small chain around her neck. It was a gift from Delilah. She knew how much her grandmother misplaced her glasses. She slowly slid them on and began to read.

November 19th

Hey ya'll! It's big Lilah! That's the new nickname Jenny gave me. She said my ass is getting too big. She thinks I've been eating too much fried chicken, but anyway, I think I still got it goin' on. I'm getting a personal trainer next week. So, Drama, Drama! The chick that got shot in the face is suing Big Rock for like a zillion dollars. He is super stressed. You know, sometimes I wonder if it's cheaper to just pay these people or pay these lawyers! Anyway, I'm still having

problems getting my money from Intersound. Tito told Jenny

that if I decide to "see" him again, he'd give me anything.

Please, and be another one of his on the side hoes! He'll

never get it again! Jenny is so upset with this whole

situation. She says we might have to sue. Sometimes it seems

like she is more worried about my problems than I am. I

asked her if she needed a break, but she insisted on

continuing to help me. She said she would never leave my

side, especially now. Rock is pissed too because we need the

money badly. He and Tito got into a shouting match and

security kicked him out. Rock has been pretty nice to me

recently. We went to Lake Tahoe and hung out, just him and

me. He loves to play Black Jack. So he did that and I played

the slot machines. It was cool. We stayed in a nice hotel. It

had a movie theater, a club, a nice pool, and of course, the

casino. We didn't really get to see too much of the hotel. Big

Rock was slamming my head against the headboard most of

the time (in a good way!!) The rest of the time we were just

talking, reminiscing on all the times we had. It felt strange to

actually feel that close to someone. It is definitely the closest

I have ever felt to any man. It was unbelievable. We had a lot

of fun. A LOT OF FUN!

Oh! I almost forgot. I was in my first movie last

month. I played the lead female role. It was a cool little film

based on a best selling book called "Pimpstress". I won't

spoil the surprise. I got the part by accident. I read for the

lead role of another movie. I didn't get that part, but the

casting director remembered me, she called my agent and I

was in. I never even expected it. It was kind of strange. My

grandmother says that when you keep pushing for what you

want, you sort of end up in the right place at the right time.

She says that other people call that luck, but they don't see

the hard work that you put in before. I think it makes sense.

Everyone is saying that I have natural acting skills. One

magazine said I had great sex appeal. One of those papers

said I needed work. They said that I should stick to my day job. Idiots! It pisses me off when people hate on me. I understand them not liking the film, but sometimes they take it too far. It really sounded personal. I usually don't put so much weight on what critics say, but sometimes I think they don't realize that I am a human being with feelings. It isn't fair for them to attack me as a person. Those stupid critics don't understand how hard it is sometimes to be a performer, I'd like to see them stand up in front of thirty thousand people singing, or act in a movie. It's easy to hide behind a pen and a desk. You know?

And to top it all off, that punk ass, so-called father of mine, Arnold, won't leave me alone. He keeps on trying, he sent me a bunch of flowers and a card to my show in Houston last week. I don't know why, but I read the card. It said something about how I wanted it when I was a little girl and I'm still the same little slut. My hands started shaking and I vomited all over the floor. I cried so hard that I gave myself a splitting migraine, but I still had to do the show. My

legs were shaking. I couldn't believe he sent that to me. I'm

his daughter for cryin' out loud, his only fuckin' daughter!

Some people in this world are just so sick. How could he not

understand that what he did was fuckin' sick? What the fuck

is wrong with him? I'm his daughter. Why? I never did

anything to him to deserve that. I don't even know him! Why

won't he just go away? Jenny says we'll file for a restraining

order, but I don't want the press to find out.

On top of that, KB told Big Rock that if he can't have

me, nobody will. What's going on? Sometimes I feel like I'm

about to have a heart attack! I can't deal with all this

pressure. I can't sleep at night, I can't concentrate, I think

I'm losing it. Plus, my grandma is getting sicker. She can

hardly remember things. I need to get my money so I can get

her a nurse aid. I worry about her so much. People from the

church come by to take care of her, but I still worry. I'm

thinking about quitting this whole business and going back to school. This business definitely is not what I thought it would be. Some days I feel like I wouldn't trade it for the world, then other days, I really wonder.

KB wrote me a long letter, I don't know why, but I read it. It wasn't really mean. He talked about the good times we had. It made me reminisce. He said I was stupid for being with Big Rock. It hit me kind of hard because it made me think, what if I really am stupid? If I wasn't a pop star, Big Rock, Tito, none of these men would want me so much. I love Rock so much, but then he is a rap star. Who am I kidding? Who knows what he could be doing behind my back. We ain't together all of the time. He is so sweet, so smart, and so talented. His ambition is so sexy, I don't know. That basketball player from the All Star Game, Rick Jonathan, called my voicemail a few times, but I don't know. Anyway, I gotta get ready for the Rucker game. Big Rock got his own team. So, I'll holla back soon One luv,. -Lilah

Ms. Brown's heart sank to her feet. It had never occurred to the grandmother that Delilah had been going through so much. That kid always kept such a tough exterior, such a confidence about her. It kind of hurt to think that protecting her feelings would stop young Delilah from being open and honest with her. She really wished she could strangle Arnold, Lord forgive her. How Ms. Brown wished she could have been someone that poor little girl could have turned to her in her time of need. All these years of experience, all those gray hairs, for nothing.

It almost seemed like a tragedy that a grandma couldn't have noticed that so many things were going wrong. Melinda felt like a complete failure. She had dropped the ball. This time there was no fixing it. It was the difference between life and death.

Knock, Knock! The sound at the door startled Melinda. Who could it be at this hour? Melinda wondered as she stood to her feet and headed for the door.

"Who is it?" She asked through the door.

The voice on the other side sounded familiar. "It's me, Elijah."

"Who is Elijah?"

"Detective Elijah Scott, ma'am."

"Oh, just a minute." Ms. Brown pulled her sweater tight. It had already been over a week since they first visited. She hoped this man had some good news. The person that did this to Delilah needed to be in prison. No sense in allowing a killer to roam free.

She slowly removed the chain and pulled the door open. "Detective Scott, found anything?"

Dr. Scott's exhausted eyes stared blankly for a second. He had been working on this case day and night. When he wasn't on the job, he was thinking about it over and over. He had been through every possible angle, every detail. Still nothing could have prepared him for what had just happened. He didn't even step inside of the house.

"Well, aren't you going to come in Detective Scott?" The two awkwardly made eye contact.

"No." Dr. Scott answered. "I just wanted to inform you of the latest events before you heard it on the news. I feel you at least deserve that."

Ms. Brown stood in complete confusion. "What's going on? What happened?"

Det. Scott sighed. "Well, Mrs. Brown, At six o'clock this morning, your daughter's boyfriend, Big Rock was shot three times in the head at his recording studio."

"Oh my God!" Melinda screamed.

"Ma'am, we don't know what's going on. My guess is he had to have known the person who did it because he buzzed them up from the intercom."

"Any witnesses?"

"No one saw anything as usual." Det. Scott's frustration was obvious. He paced Ms. Brown's front stoop like a maniac.

Melinda just stood there in the doorway with her hands covering her mouth in disbelief. Whoever these people were, they were ruthless.

Det. Nilo couldn't believe his own ears. A woman named Martha, who was a police informant, had a sister who was a clerk for a federal judge in Manhattan. Martha owed Nilo a few favors for letting her slide on theft charges many years ago. When she called his office at eleven o'clock in the morning, he was glad to hear from her. However, when she spilled the beans, he was more than glad. Martha had informed him that a federal grand jury had been convened to investigate Tito Diez and Intersound Records for violating FCC laws. The government suspected that Intersound was paying radio stations under the table to play their artists' music. Det. Nilo knew that this "payola", as it was called, was nothing new. Even though the laws were on the books, they were rarely enforced. When the Feds tried to go after record companies in the 70's, it was a complete disaster.

Nevertheless, Tito and several Intersound employees could be facing prison time. Interesting enough, Delilah's records were some of the main ones in question.

Det. Nilo rushed to catch Det. Scott on his cell. This was something that could change their entire investigation.

Det. Scott was completely perplexed after getting the call from Det. Nilo. What would this have to do with Delilah, she was just a recording artist? Where did Big Rock fit into this whole mess? He checked out all of Jenny's financial records and she was squeaky clean. It seemed that Delilah was a smart girl by trusting her friend so much. Jenny kept meticulously accurate records, down to fifty-cent lollipop purchases.

Intersound should have been ashamed of themselves for the way they treated their star artist. This girl should have been filthy, stinking rich. She didn't even have a life insurance policy.

Det. Scott looked at his watch. It was three p.m. The day was still young. Sandra Bullion, the woman who was shot in the face at Club Cheetah, was meeting him for lunch in ten minutes. The smart detective picked a small, quiet diner on Bay Chester Avenue in the Bronx. It was a good place to remain low-key. He had a feeling that this case was coming together, piece by piece.

The Intersound headquarters were packed with news cameras and microphones as the media swarmed as if in a frenzy. Everybody smelled a big story and wanted to be the first to break it. Rappers being gunned down, singers dying in mysterious automobile accidents and a crooked label! It was too good to be true for the news.

Detectives Scott and Nilo eased their way into the room as Diez and his lawyer addressed the endless questions.

"Mr. Diez, Mr. Diez? Is it true that you're a suspect in an ongoing investigation surrounding Delilah Brown's death?" A polite redhead asked.

"Mr. Diez has no comment at this time." Diez's lawyer answered for him.

"Is Big Rock's death connected to Delilah's?" The redhead reporter persistently tried to pursue the issue.

"Look, I didn't call this press conference to discuss the unfortunate demise of Big Rock or Delilah, I simply called it to ensure the public that Intersound is targeted unjustly. At no time have any executives or employees at Intersound engaged in any questionable acts to get our records played, nor do we ever intend to."

Det. Scott could see the sweat bubbling under Diez's collar as reporters fired question after question at him. From the corner of his eye, Scott saw someone trying to get his attention. He looked and saw it was Diez's accountant, Yantsen. He was trying to be discrete, but he was clearly agitated. Once he and Det. Scott made eye contact, Yantsen walked out the door. Det. Scott took it as a sign to follow him. He tapped Det. Nilo, and the two detectives left Diez and his lawyer to handle the media circus. Once out in the hallway, they saw Yantsen duck into the bathroom and they followed him. A middle aged Spanish cat was on his way out. Once he left, Det. Scott spoke up. "I assume you wanted to talk to us?"

Yantsen lit up a Marlboro and began to pace nervously. Det. Scott watched the pasty complexioned man. He looked as if he hadn't seen the sun in months. He was the poster boy of accountants and Scott wondered how he ended up working for a sleaze like Diez.

"I never asked for this. Never." Yantsen began to rattle off outloud to himself.

"I tried to tell Tito, but he wouldn't listen, I tried but."

Nilo cut him off. "What the hell are you talking about? If you got something to say, say it!"

Yantsen looked up at Nilo. "I can't go to jail. Do you know what they do to guys like me in jail?"

172

Det. Nilo had to stifle a laugh, imagining Yantsen in a pair of tight prison blues, calling some big black buffoon daddy. Instead, he replied. "I can just imagine. Now, you wanna tell us what could land you in jail?"

Yantsen glanced around nervously. "Not here, but soon, real soon. I'm privileged to certain information that I think could be very helpful to your investigation of Delilah Brown's murder."

Det. Nilo's ears perked up. "Start talking!"

"Not here, I...."

Det. Nilo lunged at Yantsen and pinned him to the wall. "Yes here and yes now!"

"You little shit, I can see you now bent the fuck over some jailhouse sink with twelve inches of gorilla sausage in your ass! You start talking or so help me I'll...."

Yantsen all but broke down in tears.

"You don't understand! It's the files, I have to get you the files! Once I get you them, you'll know. But please, you gotta help me! I'll do whatever you say, just don't let me

go to jail!"

Det. Scott tapped Det. Nilo on his shoulder. He knew

Yantsen would be putty in their hands, so there was no need

to keep the pressure up. Det. Nilo relented. "I want those

files pronto, you hear? Pronto!"

Yansten nodded like an imbecile. On the way out,

Yansten added. "Once you know what I know, you'll see

what I'm talking about. I think this information will prove

that Diez had Delilah killed."

Det. Scott couldn't wait to get his hands on those

files.

Chapter 8

Melinda fixed herself a turkey sandwich with a tall glass of Pepsi. She knew she had to lay off of the soft drinks because of her diabetes, but she just had to have it. She said a silent prayer for Big Rock's family. That poor little boy. He was a sweet, handsome child. He seemed to have made Delilah very happy. It was so strange how Detective Scott paced back and forth for a few minutes, then jumped in his car and sped off. That man seemed strange. She hoped that the police department knew what they were doing by assigning him to the case. Melinda's eyes ached from the strain, but she knew she had to keep reading her granddaughter's diary. She had to find out what happened. The old woman massaged her eyelids, then took a bite of her sandwich. She washed it down with a sip of her ice-cold Pepsi. After sliding on her reading glasses, she opened Delilah's diary. After finding her bookmark, she continued to read.

April 10th

Hey ya'll. Man, things have been crazy. I'm sorry it took so long for me to write. This whacked out schedule is hurtin' me! I got to say it is a lot of work. I've been working out with my little basketball friend, Rick Jonathan. He is getting me back in shape fast. Thank goodness! I'm killin' these heffers when I walk into the room! They are hating it! But anyway, he is such a sweet guy. He is real intelligent, nice, and FINE! And did I say FINE? Okay, well we are just friends for now. Me and Big Rock are trying to work things out. I caught him with that dancer chick alone in his trailer on the video set it's a long story.

The idiot must have forgotten that I was coming at 10 instead of 12. That's all that smoking. The little bitch had my man's dick in her mouth when I walked in! Un-fuckin- believable! She was butt naked on the floor. I had seen hoes throw their panties on the stage at him, I had heard all the stories of threesomes in hotel rooms and limos, but I never seen it with my own eyes .The groupie thing was always a problem. After the shows, they were always waiting backstage or in the hotel lobby. They always had on their cheesy fits, ass hangin' out, just waiting to fuck my man. This little fake ass dancin' bitch actually got me. But anyway, I caught his cheating behind. I beat the hell out of the little tramp. He definitely wasn't getting off the hook. I punched him dead in the face. Know what I'm saying? My hand still hurts!

It's been two months. He called me constantly for a month, I don't know. Jenny says I'm stupid, but I'm thinking about giving him another chance. Maybe he was just trippin' and forgot what we had. People make mistakes. I can't lie and say that I don't miss him. We were so good together. Sometimes I think maybe it was my fault. Maybe I wasn't paying him enough attention, maybe I criticized and complained too much, or maybe he just didn't trust me. You know, those sluts out there make it hard for women like me. Men just don't trust us sometimes. But anyway, we'll see, Jenny says not to do it. I still can't believe that I actually saw it with my own eyes. What in the fuck could she have that I don't have? What on earth could that wopped up bitch do for my man that I can't do! I swear, I don't understand men. He had everything he needed right there when he needed it. I did everything I could possibly do to make him happy. How could he repay me by sticking his dick in that tramp's face?

This is unbelievable. I feel so betrayed, better yet, I feel stupid, downright stupid.

Oh! I wrote KB a letter. I told him everything that's been going on. He wants me to go with Rick Jonathan. He said he has a good cross over. He is so silly. He sent me some of his rap lyrics, he is pretty good. It's amazing that we have become friends after all of that drama. Even though I felt like I hated him, the truth is, I will always love him. That's what made me hate him. He's still real protective over me, but he knows he has too much prison time for us to be together. I feel so bad for him sometimes. It really isn't fair. KB really does not like Big Rock. He says he dances around on the TV screen on videos like he's gay. I was dying laughing! I know that's messed up, but it's kind of true. I'm so confused. It seems like every man in my life is either a crook, a con artist, or a cheater. Jenny says I need to start going to church to meet good men, but KB says that's where you go to find the crooks! Anyway, I'm going to court with

Big Rock tomorrow. I told him that I should be allowed to call him Aaron without him getting pissed. He hates that name. His mom even calls him Big Rock. Court tomorrow is about that lady, Sandra Bullion, who filed a lawsuit against him and Intersound. Well, I'll holla back in a few. I'm going to the movies with Rick. I have to wear a disguise! How crazy! I still have to get ready and call Jenny before I go. She's always worrying. I told her not to worry, me and Rick are JUST FRIENDS!

Ms. Brown smiled brighter than the Big Dipper. Her granddaughter was so forgiving. To imagine that she would even communicate with KB after all he put her through was amazing. Melinda couldn't conceive being able to forgive Big Rock if she were Delilah. That granddaughter of hers had a gigantic heart. That was her problem. She loved and trusted too easily. In the end, it may have been what took her life. What a price to pay for being naïve. Ms. Brown decided to crash on the couch for a little power nap. She decided she would finish the book later and give it to Det. Scott. She was dead tired.

Det. Scott smiled as Sandra approached him. She was a pleasant looking girl, aside from the huge scar on her right cheek. However, the young girl seemed at peace with the ugly mark, as if it didn't exist. Det. Scott figured that she had just grown accustomed to it. It was amazing what human beings could adapt to when they had no choice.

The detective stood to his feet once she reached the table. "Hello, Ms. Bullion." He extended a handshake.

She shook his hand and smiled passively.

"Would you like something to eat, Sandra?"

"No thanks." She grinned politely.

Scott opened his menu. "Are you sure? I heard they make a mean grilled cheese sandwich."

Sandra sighed nervously. "No sir. I'd like to get this over with. My lawyers don't know I'm here. I shouldn't be doing this."

"I understand." Det. Scott answered. "Just know that this is all completely off the record."

Sandra nodded. "It better be, Det. Scott. I don't even know why I'm doing this."

"You are doing this because you are a good person. You know that someone lost their life and you want to help."

Sandra cut her eyes. "Listen detective. To be honest with you, I'm glad the little tramp is dead!"

Det. Scott was shocked. "What?"

Sandra thrust her face within an inch of Det. Scott's nose. She made sure that he got a good look. "Do you see my face?"

Det. Scott nodded nervously. Sandra's voice grew louder. "Do you see my face!"

"Yes, Sandra. I see your face."

People in the diner started to stare at the scene she was causing but she didn't care. "Do you know what it feels like to be called the elephant woman? Do you know my boyfriend left me for a cheerleader! My dog is even scared of me!"

Det. Scott whispered uncomfortably, "It really isn't that bad Sandra."

"That's easy for you to say. All I did was go out and try to have a good time for New Year's Eve. I didn't deserve a bullet just because someone had to prove a point."

"Prove a point?" Det. Scott asked, not understanding.

"Yeah, the point that Big Rock is some kind of gangster, somebody who's hard!"

"Sandra, who did he have to prove it to?"

Sandra rolled her eyes at the detective. "What are you an idiot? I thought you guys knew stuff!"

Det. Scott leaned closer. 'Stuff like what?"

"Come on man!" Sandra laughed in astonishment.

Det. Scott leaned in even closer. "Tell me what I am so stupid for not knowing, Sandra."

Sandra slapped her hands on the table. "Everybody knows that little slut used to mess with KB, and he don't play that!"

"What do you mean?"

Sandra rolled her eyes again and sighed. "Big Rock is a wanna-be, KB is the real thing!"

Det. Scott was confused. "Real thing?"

"Yes, the real thing, a thug."

Det. Scott wished this girl would get to the point. "So what does that mean Sandra?"

"Well detective, that little floozy was sleeping with that whack rapper, and she left a gangster with a broken heart, you figure it out. Then, the whack rapper was flossin' her on his videos."

"Flossin'?" Det. Scott didn't know the slang.

Sandra smacked her teeth. "Showing her off!"

Det. Scott finally caught on. "Okay, so KB sent a hit because of jealousy."

Sandra moved her head from side to side as she spoke. "Man, he sent more than a hit. He sent Pinky Blades, another gangster!"

Det. Scott scratched his head. "Well, that's what we thought might have happened."

Sandra stood. "Well it did. It happened, and it happened to my face. What other evidence do you need? Or do you want my hospital bills?"

"No, that won't be necessary."

Sandra turned on her heels and walked out. "Stupid cops." She mumbled.

Det. Scott was happy to receive confirmation of what he already believed had happened, but now he had more questions. Was Sandra a possible suspect? Did KB finish the job of killing Big Rock? Did KB order a hit on Delilah? Where was Pinky Blades?

Ring. Ring!

Det. Scott snapped open his cell phone. It was Nilo.

"Hey partner." Det. Nilo yelled into the static, he was barely audible.

"What ya got?" Det. Scott was still in thought.

"Well, I got what you call a mess. They found our friend Pinky Blades in a dumpster in Marcy with fifteen donut holes in his back."

Det. Scott was speechless.

Nilo continued. "We've got forensics, homicide, the works. Captain says the Feds are on their way. Too much heat."

"Damn." Det. Scott hated when those arrogant federal agents messed up his investigations. Those cheap suit-wearing logs on the road wouldn't know police work if it smacked them in the face. He hated the Feds. He thought that this was a bad dream already, now it was a nightmare.

After almost two weeks passed since the FBI entered the investigation, Det. Scott felt like he was in a living hell. Those arrogant fools complained about everything and they loved to criticize. Scott was reluctant to share his information with them. The captain had scolded him twice already.

Det. Nilo had been doing a wonderful job. He had checked into the payola scandal involving Diez. He found out that the Feds did want to pursue the case, but the grand jury refused to issue an indictment. Diez was a very powerful and respected man. If you wanted to pin him with something, you had to really have him nailed, so that was a dead end. Having sex with Delilah at a young age was illegal, but how could they prove that? Could Diez have had Delilah killed in fear of his indictment? Was it an effort to stop her from testifying? How could they prove it?

Dr. Scott ran KB's words through his mind over and over. "Gangsters want to be rappers and rappers want to be gangsters. What did it mean?" He glanced at his watch. It was 2:17 p.m. The cold winter wind in New York City was punishing at this time of year. He was supposed to meet

Sasha, Delilah's old group member, at two o'clock. She was late.

Det. Scott felt uncomfortable outside of the train station on Gun Hill Road in the Bronx. He had busted a lot of drug dealers around here when he was on the mayor's narcotics taskforce. He would hate to be recognized while out here alone. He tapped his nine-millimeter Smith and Wesson under his coat to reassure himself. He lit a cigarette and let the cool smoke blow into the chilly breeze.

As he watched people walking back and forth in every direction, it reminded him of how life goes on. People were doing their laundry, heading home from school, thinking about life's menial aspects. No one cared that Delilah had lost her life. People were thinking about cashing their checks or getting a slice of pizza, life just went on. It was a little painful to think of how the world can just keep going.

"Mr. Scott." The detective was shaken from deep thought by Sasha's voice.

"Mr. Scott, I'm sorry I'm late. I had to get this little bugaboo dressed." Sasha said.

Det. Scott looked down at Sasha's two-year-old son. "Handsome little bugaboo isn't he?"

"Do you want to take him for a few days?" She joked.

Det. Scott smiled. "Are you hungry?"

"No I'm fine." Scott put his cigarette out and stomped on it. "Let's walk and talk." He said, while blowing the last pull out of his nose.

Sasha walked along slowly, pulling the young boy's arm in frustration. "So, what do you need from me?" Sasha asked, as if she was in a rush. She didn't seem to be exactly thrilled about talking to Det. Scott.

"Well, Sasha." The detective said as he lit another cigarette.

"You need to let those things go. They kill." Sasha interrupted.

"We all gotta go sometime." Det. Scott smirked while lighting up. "What do I want from you?" He continued. "Tell me about Delilah."

Sasha fidgeted a little and then answered. "Well, we all grew up together not to far from here, me, Jenny and Lilah. We were best friends. We had a little group together, but to make a long story short, the two of them ditched me here and never came back."

"Well, didn't you refuse to talk to them?"

Sasha nodded. "Yeah, but they knew where to find me if they really wanted to. They only cared about themselves. Then she ran off with that rapper. How stupid can you be? Now she's dead."

Det. Scott looked confused. "What does that mean?"

"Well, do you really think she would be dead if she hadn't got involved with that gay rapper, his shootouts and all that stupidity?"

Det. Scott noticed that Sasha referred to Big Rock as "gay". KB used the same word in describing him.

"Kendo! No!" Sasha yelled at her son, as he was wandering off.

Det. Scott couldn't help but notice that Kendo was also KB's real name. His detective intuition had kicked in.

"Tell me about KB." He said.

Sasha's eyes grew wide. She stumbled over her words for a second, and then replied. "He's a good man. He just got a bad rap. The Feds set him up. He didn't deserve what Delilah did to him."

"What did she do?" Det. Scott asked.

"She turned her back on him. She made him look bad."

Det. Scott knew by the look on her face that she cared for KB. He didn't have to ask. "So, is KB involved in any of this?" Det. Scott asked.

"I don't know." She shifted her eyes away from Det. Scott.

"Look Sasha, your personal life isn't my business. Is KB involved?"

"No." Sasha began to cry. "He loved her. He started writing me. We flirted a little while they were together, but I never let him touch me. He has a lot of years to do. It happened in the visiting room. I felt bad for him. It had been years since he touched a woman. I let him do me in the visiting room. I just pulled up my skirt right there. I cared about him. He's all alone out there. That's how I had lil KB."

"Did Delilah know?" Det. Scott asked.

Sasha wiped her face. "I don't want him to see me crying." She looked down at her son and continued. "I tried to call her the morning she died. I wanted to tell her, but it was too late."

"Why did you wait so long?"

"They left me here, detective. They left me here while they traveled around the world pursuing our dream! You don't think it hurt me to see her on TV? To have to buy a ticket to see her perform!"

Det. Scott touched her shoulder.

Sasha pulled away. "Do you know what it feels like to always feel second to someone else? Do you?" She asked, as tears streamed down her cheeks.

"Not really." Det. Scott responded.

"Well it hurts. Even with my son's father I was second, second to Delilah. She always had to be the center of attention no matter what. She had to have it all. That's why I sent the report about her being molested to the radio station."

Det. Scott looked away. "Sasha, do you know who killed Delilah? I'm only gonna ask you once."

"Yes." She answered.

Det. Scott grabbed her by the shoulders. "Who?"

Sasha looked deep into the detective's eyes. "Delilah," She said. "Delilah killed herself with her own stupidity!"

Det. Scott exhaled. He heard enough. "I'll be in touch." He said as he walked away. "Get that kid out of the street!" He yelled.

With friends like that, enemies could take the week off.

Chapter 9

The Federal Correctional Institution in Texarkana was the site of total pandemonium. KB was on the ground in a small holding cell in the Special Housing Unit, which was commonly referred to as the "hole". Inmates were usually sent there after breaking the rules, but KB hadn't gotten into any trouble. They woke him up at four o'clock in the morning and brought him there, but he didn't know why. He arrived in handcuffs and was greeted by four FBI agents. They didn't give their names. After four hours of interrogation and being hit in the face with a phone book, KB could take no more.

"We know you did it!" One of the agents hollered. "We found Pinky Blades in the dumpster with the gun. The bullets matched the ones that killed Big Rock!"

"So what!" KB screamed. Blood spewed everywhere each time he tried to talk.

"We found the encoded letter in his pocket. We matched your handwriting, you prick!"

KB fell to the ground as one of the agents kicked him in the chest.

"We know you ordered the hits! Tell us why you did it!"

"I ain't saying nothin'!" KB couldn't believe how stupid Pinky was. How could he have been so careless? He knew he couldn't trust Pinky as much because of that drug problem, but that pea brain had basically sunk him.

"Did you order the hit on Delilah?" Another agent yelled, as he kicked the prisoner in the ribs.

"Kill me." KB responded in a raspy whisper.

"Don't tempt us." One of the other agents replied. "You ordered Pinky Blades dead, but only after he did your dirt!"

"Detective Scott." KB mumbled. "I'll only talk to Detective Scott."

After another hour of beatings and unanswered questions, an agent grabbed his cell phone and began dialing Det. Scott's number. "You better not be wasting my time." The agent warned as the phone rang.

Rick Jonathan was exhausted. He had just scored thirty-three points against the Pacers. It was always a physical game against that team. His ribs ached and so did the soles of his feet. He was glad to grab a shower and be on his way home. However, his heart was in worse shape than his body. He still hadn't completely gotten over Delilah's death. Losing her was devastating to him. He considered leaving basketball all together. How could he play with so much depression?

He stopped his Benz next to a gas station. He searched through the phone book for the New York Police Department. After a few minutes, he found the number to the homicide division. He was glad he decided to hire that private investigator. It was worth it. Now all he had to do was find the detective in charge of Delilah's case. He missed her so much, it was hard to function. He hoped that helping to solve her murder would give him some closure.

Nilo was tired of the news stories. It had now been over a month since Delilah's death. Everybody had an opinion about what happened to her. These conspiracy theorists drove him up the wall. He couldn't wait to solve this case by himself and make everyone look silly. Especially those stuck up federal agents. They had no business sticking their noses in this investigation anyway.

Det. Nilo would show Det. Scott which one of them was the key player on the team. He was the reason why the captain considered them the best on the force for this case. It sure wasn't Scott's smooth approach and razor sharp instincts, it was Nilo's brawn. He immersed himself in Delilah's financial records. Come on Delilah, he thought to himself, tell me something.

Det. Scott was appalled to be getting a call this early in the morning. Who on earth could it be? He had been up all night working on the case. He needed some serious sleep. As he awoke, it suddenly dawned on him that he was all alone. He kind of wished someone were next to him. His apartment was so plain and empty, and his life was in the same condition. He grabbed his ringing cell phone in frustration.

"Who in heaven's name is this?" He asked.

"Detective Scott?" The federal agent in the small holding cell with KB asked.

"Yes, this is he. Do you know what time it is?"

"Well." The federal agent said. "Unlike the NYPD, the FBI don't sleep."

"What the hell do you want." Det. Scott snarled.

"Someone wants to speak to you."

KB waited for the agent to finish briefing Det. Scott.

"We found some of your little inmate friend's rap lyrics here. He describes the crimes he committed exactly."

After the rest of the details of their evidence were given, the phone was shoved into KB's face. A drop of blood dripped on the agent's hand as he held the phone to KB's ear.

"Scott." KB said, in a menacing voice.

The detective was absolutely floored. How did the Feds beat him to the punch? He was so angry at himself for letting them crack the case open. Now they would be on TV taking all of the credit.

"Son." Det. Scott said. "Why did you do it?"

"Delilah wrote me and told me everything. I did it for her. Nobody hurts her and gets away with it."

"Did you order the club hit KB?"

"I did it to protect Delilah."

"Did you kill Delilah, KB?"

"Never."

Det. Scott was on the edge of his bed. "Son, if you talk to me, I can help you. You're in a lot of trouble." He said

"I would never hurt Delilah. Naw, never that!"

Det. Scott screamed into the phone. Veins were bulging from his forehead. "Well, who did it then!"

"Scott, that punk record company dude is next." KB whispered.

"What!" Det. Scott jumped up. "When!" He screamed.

"Sooner than soon." KB laughed out loud. His bloody grin was earth shattering.

"Put the agent back on the phone, you maniac!"

KB motioned to the agent. "I loved her." He mumbled, as the agent grabbed the phone.

"He's got another one in the works right now!" Det. Scott screamed.

"Well, what are you doing still on the line?" The agent rolled his eyes in disbelief.

"I'm on my way!" Det. Scott yelled.

He rushed to put on his pants. He had to call Nilo. They needed some squad cars over at Intersound, right away. It was already early morning.

Det. Scott's heart was racing far beyond natural speed. He had to get to Diez before the killer. This whole drama began to unfold in a way he had never dreamed of. He had to move fast. He put in the call to his partner and informed him of what was about to happen.

Det. Nilo couldn't believe his ears. He grabbed his desert eagle and a twenty-five caliber handgun and he dashed to the car. He knew he was a little closer to Times Square than Scott. He had to make it there first. If he didn't get there soon, there would be more bloodshed.

Rick Jonathan couldn't wait to find this Detective Scott. He hoped to catch him at his desk. He strolled into the precinct trying to look as calm as he possibly could. Unfortunately, his nervously shaking hands were a dead give away. He tried having Det. Scott paged at the front desk, but he wasn't in. Rick decided to sit on the wooden bench in front of the lobby and wait no matter how long it took.

Det. Nilo had sixteen squad cars trailing him to Intersound's headquarters. Sirens were blaring, horns were honking, and traffic was swerving over to the shoulder of the lane.

The army of police arrived at the record company in just a few minutes. Det. Nilo slammed on his brakes, bringing his Buick sedan to a sudden halt just in front of the building. He hopped out in a frenzy, without even bothering to shut off the engine or close the car door.

The anxious detective loaded his desert eagle and strapped his bulletproof vest on tight. Fifty police officers flanked him as they ran at top speed, guns drawn.

Half of the officers took the elevator and the other half took the stairs. Det. Nilo raced up the staircase on foot. Once he had reached the eleventh floor, he began to feel his age. "Only five more floors." He whispered through his heaving chest.

All of the people in the lobby panicked and ran as the S.W.A.T. team entered the building. Children were crying, no one knew what was going on.

Det. Nilo stood back as he slowly opened the staircase door on the sixteenth floor. He didn't know what to expect. There was no telling what was on the other side of that door. "Go, Go!" He screamed. Two officers ran into the hallway, while two other officers covered them. The remaining officers followed the same procedure, until they were all out of the stairwell.

Det. Nilo kicked open the front doors at Intersound. The police from the elevators filed in behind the others. Det. Nilo didn't understand how he could have gotten there before them, he had taken the stairs.

Det. Nilo's gun was ready to fire. His index finger trembled on the cold trigger. He moved slowly through the front lobby. He remembered where Diez's office was from their two earlier meetings. There was a weird silence across the room. Everyone was trying to move as swiftly as possible. He shook his head in dismay, while stepping over the bloody corpses of the black security guard and the skinny secretary.

Det. Nilo's entire body was on full alert as he poked his gun into Diez's office. His eyes grew wide in astonishment to what he saw.

"Freeze! Police!" He screamed. "Drop the gun!"

The rest of the squad rushed to the door. They stepped back for cover as shots were fired. The bullets ricocheted off of the walls and the sound stung Det. Nilo's ears. Det. Nilo pulled his trigger. At that moment, life moved in slow motion. Det. Nilo watched the bullet as it traveled at light speed and hit his target.

By this time, Det. Scott had run into the office, backed by the S.W.A.T. team. The armored police officers pushed past everyone with authority. They entered the room with force and pounced on top of Det. Nilo's target.

Det. Nilo stood there speechless. As his target fell to the floor, he prayed that the worst would not happen. He had never actually taken a life. He had been on the force for fourteen years, and he never had to kill anyone. He felt numb all over. What made it worse, was that he was too late, he didn't stop the murder from taking place. If he only had arrived a second earlier.

Everyone was screaming, police were running frantically towards the office. Det. Nilo stood there in disbelief. Det. Scott couldn't conceive intellectually what his eyes were showing him. Sasha had shot Diez in the face and Nilo had shot Sasha in the stomach.

Sasha kicked and screamed violently as the cops held her down on the ground.

Diez's body lay motionless. He was definitely not going to make it. Det. Scott didn't understand why KB would send Sasha. As he thought about it, it became clear to him. Sasha had his child. She loved him. She would have done anything for him.

Paramedics stormed into the office and took one look at Diez and realized he was dead. They went to work on Sasha, they began to rip Sasha's clothes off. It was a horrible scene, the sleek black carpet was now smothered in burgundy blood.

Det. Scott knelt beside the girl. The paramedics tried to push him back but he wouldn't budge. "Sasha." He said. "Did you kill Pinky Blades too?"

Sasha knew she was about to die. She didn't know why she let KB push her into this. She promised herself that she wouldn't let him take advantage of her again. KB had promised her that he would take care of little KB. He told her that he had a million dollars stashed in his grandmother's back yard. All she had to do was take care of Pinky Blades and Diez and she could have it. So, she did it. She never thought it would cost her life.

"Please." Sasha whispered painfully. "Please promise me you'll make sure my son is okay."

Det. Scott nodded.

"Promise me!" She yelled, with as much force as she could muster.

"I promise." Det. Scott answered. The detective noticed the dark blood oozing from the young girl's midsection. Det. Scott was no doctor, but he knew that a major

artery had been severed. This girl didn't have much time.

Sasha winced as they lifted her up onto the stretcher.

"I killed Pinky Blades." She said. "KB knew he was trouble,

he was on drugs, too sloppy. Diez had it coming also."

Det. Scott ran along side the stretcher. "Who killed

Delilah?" He yelled.

"I don't know." Sasha whispered. "I loved her."

The paramedics whisked Sasha away. By the looks

on their faces, Det. Scott knew she wouldn't make it.

Love was a crazy thing. KB wasn't lying when he

said he would kill for Delilah. The worst thing was, once the

prosecutors got a hold of this case, they would seek the death

penalty for KB. In the end, he actually killed himself. All of

the pieces of the puzzle were coming together except for the

main one, Delilah's murderer.

Chapter 10

Both Detectives Nilo and Scott frowned as they saw the flurry of federal agents enter the building. Of course, they always tugged the media. The two partners decided to get back to the office and strategize.

Det. Nilo was still a little shaken up. Det. Scott was baffled. He made a note for himself to personally call Child Protective Services for little KB. This complex web of murderous passion was frightening. Where did Delilah fit in? There was still something missing. They had to find it, and it had to happen before the Feds could steal their case.

Melinda turned up the volume on the television so she could hear the six o'clock news. She couldn't believe the words coming out of the anchorman's mouth. She just could not believe the reports about KB, Big Rock, Mr. Diez and little Sasha. This whole situation was a lot wilder than she had imagined.

The reporter made her remember when Delilah was on the news. She remembered the shootout at the club on New Year's Eve. How could she have forgotten? She saw KB's face on the screen. He was such a nice young boy. Delilah had him over at the house many nights. She couldn't understand how all of their lives had collided in a pool of blood. The worst part about it was that Delilah's life was lost in the crash. She held back her emotions. She had enough of the crying. Melinda turned down the volume and picked up her granddaughter's diary.

Det. Scott blazed past Rick Jonathan on his way to his office. Nilo followed closely on his heels. Both men seemed completely frantic. Scott's mind was on the missing link that he couldn't seem to find.

Det. Nilo could only think of the mountain of paper work that awaited him. You couldn't just use deadly force and walk away. There were tons of reports to write and questions to answer. Luckily, the detectives dodged the squadron of hungry reporters outside of the crime scene.

"Mr. Scott!" Ricky called. "Mr. Scott!"

Det. Scott stopped in his tracks. "Yes, may I help you?"

Rick stood. "My name is Rick Jonathan, sir."

Det. Nilo smiled. "Wait a minute. You play for the Knicks!"

Rick smiled. "Yes sir."

Det. Nilo's face lit up in excitement. "You scored thirty against the Bulls last week!"

Rick nodded. "Yes sir, I did."

Det. Scott hated sports. His mind was definitely on other things. "How can I help you son?"

Rick looked around. "Can we talk in private?" He asked in a boyish tone. "It's about Delilah Brown."

"Come into my office."

The three men moved past the lobby and up a flight of dusty stairs to Det. Scott's stockpile of an office. The hectic pace of the filthy station was unnerving.

Rick was slightly disgusted by the two detectives. Their suits were dirty and cheap and they reeked of cigarette smoke and donuts. He couldn't believe that these were the people that the state hired to find Delilah's killer. No wonder the Feds had to jump in.

"Have a seat." Det. Scott said.

Nilo sat beside the both of them and unbuttoned his coat. His leg was shaking uncontrollably. It was a nervous habit he had when he was under a terrible amount of stress. Det. Nilo reached into his pocket and popped a Xanax pill into his mouth. His psychiatrist told him to take one twice a day, but he helped himself to at least four.

As the men took their seats, a uniformed officer handed Det. Scott a Federal Express package.

"Thank you." He said nonchalantly. He began opening the package before checking to see who sent it. After glancing at the sender, he looked at Det. Nilo. "It's from the accounting guy, Yantsen, at Intersound."

Det. Nilo rolled his eyes.

Det. Scott peeked up at Rick. "So, Mr. Basketball, what cha got?"

Rick ignored the sarcasm and began to answer.

Det. Scott, while reading the contents of the package, motioned for his partner to step outside of the office for a second. Rick Jonathan waited patiently.

"Nilo." He said coldly, once they were out of Rick's listening range. "You gotta see this. It says that this package contains proof that they embezzled three million from Delilah!"

Det. Nilo was shocked. "Who?"

"Look!"

Det. Nilo scampered closer to Scott and began to read. "You don't say!" He exclaimed as his eyes moved a mile a minute. Nilo kept reading. "Look here, it also says that Big Rock and his label were to be dropped because of the lawsuit from Sandra Bullion and for payola by Big Rock that kicked off the federal investigation of Intersound. He owed Diez six million dollars!"

"This is big." Det. Scott said. "This is big!"

The two detectives tried to contain themselves. They decided to head back into the office and see what information Rick had.

Once the detectives re-entered, Rick Jonathan leaned forward in his seat. "You've got to hear this." He said nervously.

Both of the detectives stared at him. "What?" They asked in unison.

Rick Jonathan squirmed for a second. He wondered if he should trust these guys. The tall, lanky basketball player pulled a wad of folded documents out of his back pocket. He slowly spread them out on top of the heap of junk that Det. Scott called a desk.

Both Detectives Scott and Nilo had their eyes jolted open by surprise.

"This is a report from a private investigator that I hired to check into Delilah's situation." Rick said.

"Private investigator?" Det. Nilo was tense.

"Yeah, well she complained to me about some problems that she was having. I wanted to get to the bottom of things for her."

Det. Nilo scratched his head pensively. "You crazy, jealous prick." He fumed. "You rich guys, you think you own everything, including people!"

Rick was obviously enraged by the comment. "I was only trying to help her!" He screamed.

All of the police officers that were busy talking, joking, answering phones and moving about, suddenly stopped. They stared at the three men in complete silence.

Rick looked around. He was slightly embarrassed.

"Carry on." Det. Scott said to the crowd. "There's nothing to see here."

Everyone slowly moved back to what they were doing. A few people took a couple of extra peeks.

Rick continued. "Listen." He said while flashing a dirty look at Det. Nilo. "There were some issues with her money and that sorry rapper cheating on her. She turned to me for help. I just wanted to get the truth for her."

"So what did you find?" Det. Scott asked. He didn't have much patience for these silly love triangles anymore. This case was on the verge of being solved, he could feel it in his bones.

"Well, we found that Big Rock had chartered a plane at the John F. Kennedy airport on the morning of Delilah's murder. Delilah was not scheduled to get on that plane. It was going to Mexico. Big Rock also closed his bank account downtown, receiving two and a half million in cash that morning."

Det. Nilo leaned in a little closer. "What else?"

"Well." Rick said. "Big Rock had ordered a suite at the Hilton in Queens the day before Delilah was killed. A chummy little guy that worked in room service gave us the bill, and guess whose credit card was used for the shrimp pasta and red wine?"

"Whose?" Det. Scott asked desperately.

"Jenny Santiago."

"What!" Det. Scott couldn't believe what he was hearing.

Rick wasn't done yet. "Their limo driver called in his itinerary. He dropped Jenny off at home early that morning and dropped Big Rock off at another hotel, then picked up Delilah and headed back to Jenny's house for the trip to the airport." Rick put his head down. He didn't even want to say the words. He didn't want to say that Delilah was dead, not with the very same lips he used to kiss her so passionately so many times. To him, she was more than a Princess could ever be. She was the most amazing, compassionate human being he had ever known. He hated Big Rock and he was glad that he was killed.

"Wow!" Det. Scott said. He felt as if he was on a huge roller coaster that was spiraling to its end. He was on the edge of his seat about to spill his guts. This was a tremendous pattern of events that lead to the most tragic of outcomes. Love was a powerful emotion, one that seemed to have transformed into the deadliest form of hate.

Melinda eased back on her old sofa. Delilah had begged her to step up the elegance in her plain old home. It was almost exactly the same as it had been twenty years ago.

They painted a few times but nothing major. The light green pastel walls and the cheap linoleum floors gave it a seventies feel. The smell of home cooking still lingered in the air. There was an old, chipped, wooden china dresser against the wall, a small coffee table, and even an old eight track next to the stereo. The only modern amenity was the huge sixty-inch screen television that Delilah forced her to accept for her birthday last year.

Delilah vowed never to move out as long as her grandmother still had breath in her lungs. They had the type of relationship that only a mother and a daughter could share, or so it seemed. Melinda wished that the child could have talked to her about the horrible problems she was having. She sighed, removed her bookmark, slid on her glasses and continued to read.

May 13th

Hey ya'll. It's Lilah. Sorry it's been so long since I wrote. I've been okay. A lot of stuff has been happening. I've

221

been feeling a little guilty for kicking it with that basketball player, Rick. I've gone to a couple of his games and we've been going on dates and stuff. I hate to say it, but I still want to stay close to Big Rock. I've been going to court with him and all of that. I just don't know. I don't understand why he has to do the things that he does. Things have been so strange lately. Rock is having a problem with his artist, Lil Smooth, that went to jail because of the shootout. He is accusing Big Rock of being a snitch and he wants him dead. On top of that, there is this big federal investigation on him and Tito for paying the radio stations to play one of my songs. I can't take it no more! Tito says he is just going to drop Big Rock as an artist and keep me. Now Rock thinks I'm sleeping with Tito again.

KB is furious about everything that's been happening to me. He doesn't have it all, if you know what I mean. I think he might do something crazy! I know he is just trying to protect me because he cares about me and everything, and I care about him a lot too, but I just don't want him to go do

and anything stupid. He seems to have this illusion that he

owns me or something. I don't know.

I'm still having trouble getting my money. The

accounting guy at Intersound has been leaving me messages

all the time. I don't know why, he says it's urgent. This is the

worst thing that I've ever had to say in my life. You see, Big

Rock, as it turns out, is the one person in my life that I truly

loved, the one thing I tried to hold on to. I would give all of

this up for him in a heartbeat. I've humbled and humiliated

myself just to keep him. I've never felt so low, so small, so

powerless. That's what love can do to you sometimes. My

grandma says that love is the most powerful emotion that

God has given to us. It is stronger than hate and stronger

than pride. But sometimes I wonder if it is stronger than

greed or jealousy.

I spoke to one of the lawyers that we hired to sue

Intersound. He looked at the books. He told me the truth,

Jenny stole from me. I knew it. I know that's why that accountant guy is calling me non-stop. She's getting really crazy! She stole my trust and I think she is trying to steal my man. I see the way they look at each other, as if I'm stupid. I saw it coming. I didn't say anything about it because I just didn't want to believe it. I kept convincing myself that it wasn't true. I fired the lawyer, I can't face it. I'm gonna have a heart to heart with Jenny and find out the real. Fuck it, who am I kidding, it hurts so bad to have to see it with my own eyes. Big Rock would gawk at her like she is the best thing he has ever seen. Some friend she is, tired heifer! Every time I look in her direction, she is staring him down. I'm not stupid. Jenny forgets that underneath the furs, the hair, the makeup, and away from the cameras, I come from the same place that she does. I recognize game when I see it. It's cool. Right now, I'm keeping it cool, but I know that she knows that I know. She has become so envious of me. I am going to get some lawyers and let them get my money. I don't know what to do about everything else. So whoever is reading this, if something happens to me, God forbid, Jenny Santiago "my best friend" is who you look at first.

I feel so alone right now. I'm so sick of crying. This is the last time I'll ever shed a tear over this crap. I really wish my grandmother was here with me right now. God, she has a way of making the worst seem okay. I hope she is praying for me. I don't know why I keep crying. I gotta be strong. I feel so bad for Sasha. Turns out, she was the smartest. This whole thing is nothing like I dreamed it would be. My hands are shaking right now. I gotta go. Lilah, the so-called "Pop Diva".

Melinda was crushed. She felt like a huge avalanche full of cold sadness had fallen upon her. She searched the rest of the composition book. There were no more pages.

Detectives Scott and Nilo were dumbfounded. As soon as Rick Jonathan left, the crime scene investigators had come with their findings.

Det. Scott recognized the old, shaggy looking lieutenant that briefed them. "Gentlemen." He said. "We've finally wrapped up the findings. I thought I'd come through before the official stuff happens."

"What ya got." Det. Nilo asked.

"Well, basically we found the murder weapon a quarter mile away from the scene of the crime. It was a porcelain glock forty-five. It broke into pieces during the wreck. It took us three weeks to put it together."

Det. Nilo shot up. "Why didn't we hear about this?"

"Well, the Feds wanted everything first. They kept a tight lid on this stuff."

"What!" Det. Scott also jolted up from his chair.

"Let me finish, guys."

"Finish!" Det. Nilo screamed at the lieutenant.

"Well, we recreated the crime. The bullet in the driver's head came from behind. Delilah's bullet came from the right side. Jenny Santiago's wound was self-inflicted underneath the chin. The limo flipped over six, maybe seven times, then slid a hundred feet or so. All of the bullets match the barrel of the gun.

"Oh, my God!" Det. Scott was stunned.

"So it was Jenny!"

"She must have been psychotic or something," The lieutenant said.

"No, no." Det. Scott knew better. "She was going to kill Delilah and meet Big Rock. Then catch the flight to Mexico with two and a half million in cold hard cash. They were gonna live like king and queen with that type of money down there!"

The lieutenant nodded. "She couldn't go through with it. So, she whacked the driver and herself. What a nut job!"

Det. Scott gave his partner another one of his famous cold stares. He was so deep in thought that he couldn't even hear the rest of what the lieutenant was saying. He didn't even see him walk out.

Det. Scott knew that the Feds didn't share the information that they had because they wanted to take all the credit. But he didn't care about the credit. Everything was wrong and his heart wouldn't stop double beating. He had to see Ms. Brown. He wanted to be the one to tell her what had transpired and he wanted to do it right away.

"I'll be back." Scott mumbled to Nilo as he grabbed his coat and walked out the door. Nilo contemplated Scott's departing footsteps. Something wasn't right. The case had been wrapped up neatly, too neatly. Nilo wondered what kind of thinking would cause a girl to murder her friend in cold blood and then kill herself? For what? No one gained anything from it. If she truly loved Rock, she wouldn't have killed herself and if she couldn't have gone through with it, then she wouldn't have shot Delilah either. Sure, she had embezzled a huge sum, but why embezzle it and then not be able to spend it.

Det. Nilo looked at the Feds report once more. The wound under the chin was definitely close range. The gunpowder found around the wound proved that. He sat back and looked at a picture of Jenny and Delilah in happier times that was a part of the file. Delilah was clowning for the camera but Jenny appeared to be writing something. Det. Nilo leaned forward, wide eyed. He stared at the photo, then read the Fed report again. The report said the trajectory of the bullet was right angled but Det. Nilo could see clearly from the photo that Jenny was left-handed! Jenny hadn't killed herself, she was killed and made to look like she had killed herself.

Now it all came together for Det. Nilo, he finally understood. He picked up his coat and walked out the door. He had a killer to apprehend and he knew just where to look.

Ms. Brown slowly walked over to the VCR and pressed play. Delilah's old ballerina tape was still in there. She smiled as she watched little Delilah prancing all over the screen. She laughed as her grandbaby fell down and jumped right back up and kept dancing, it was her favorite part. She rested Delilah's book on the coffee table and prayed that she wouldn't forget to give it to Det. Scott. She was glad that pretty soon her Alzheimer's would wipe all of this intolerable pain from her memory.

Ms. Brown knew that God gives and he takes away, and he can never be questioned. She now longed for the day that he would take his breath back, out of her tired lungs. She had seen so much and she had hurt so much. She had loved so hard and lost everything that was dear to her. One thing the old woman knew for sure was that sometimes life can hit you like a tornado, twisting and turning.

Suddenly, Ms. Brown heard a knock at the door.

"Who is it?"

"It's me, Detective Scott."

She was glad he had come. She could give him the book and hopefully aid in the investigation now that she had read what Delilah had said about Jenny. Ms. Brown wobbled over to the door and let Det. Scott in.

"Praise the Lord, I'm glad you're here. I have something to give you." Ms. Brown said, opening the door.

Det. Scott watched her movements as she went to retrieve something off of the table. He felt so sorry for her loss and he was determined to bring her the much deserved answers to the questions Delilah's death had brought up. She returned with the book and handed it to him.

"What's this?" Det. Scott asked.

"Delilah's diary. I've been meaning to give it to you, but my Alzheimer's you know. I think it'll help you in your investigation. Delilah says Jenny was stealing from her, poor child."

"Yes, yes, we know." Det. Scott answered.

231

"And Delilah says Jenny also wanted her boyfriend. She says, if anything happens to her, look to Jenny."

Det. Scott paced a few feet from the door. "Yes, that's what the police think happened as well."

"Praise God! Then it's over?"

The innocence in Ms. Brown's elderly eyes made Det. Scott drop his head.

"Yes, the investigation is over. It's not being called a murder/suicide."

Ms. Brown looked at him confused. "It's not? What do you mean?"

Det. Scott turned toward the window and sighed deeply.

"Ms. Brown, you had such a lovely granddaughter, so beautiful. She was a wonderful girl. I'm sure she made you proud."

"Yes, but what did you mean that's not what happened?"

Det. Scott turned to her with tear stained eyes.

"The first time I met her was at her first album signing. She was so nice to everybody, and her smile, it lit up the room. I didn't speak to her directly, but when I did, I knew that I could I loved her."

Ms. Brown's mouth fell agape, because she knew where he was going.

"Detective, did you." Her voice trailed off. She couldn't bring herself to say anymore.

"But the industry, it was destroying her, changing her. I could see it and that Big Rock." Det. Scott spit angrily. "That bastard! He didn't love her! He didn't know her! I loved her! But she couldn't see it. The industry had her blinded. She needed me, I could've protected her from all of them, I would've died to protect her, but she rejected me!" The tears poured from Det. Scott's eyes.

Ms. Brown stared in amazement. "It was you." She said, thinking of the man Delilah was speaking of that was stalking her. She said he was security or military, but in reality he was a cop! He was Detective Scott.

"You're the one Delilah wrote about!"

Det. Scott eyes brightened psychotically. "She wrote about me? What did write? Did she love me? What did she say?"

He frantically flipped through page after page until he read where Delilah wrote about him. His smile turned to rage. "Leave her alone! She wanted a restraining order against me? You stupid bitch! I was the only man that ever loved you! But you wouldn't listen, would you? So I followed you, I followed you because I just wanted to talk. I followed the Hummer and I panicked. Oh God, I'm sorry! I'm sorry!"

Det. Scott broke down on his knees, in violent sobs. Ms. Brown didn't know what to do. "I ran the Hummer off the road, I didn't expect it to flip, I just wanted it to stop. But the driver, he saw my face. I couldn't let him see me and live. And Jenny, she was unconscious when I put the gun in her hand and raised it to her chin. I knew they'd think she did it. Then, oh Delilah, why did you make me do it? I would've loved you all my life".

Ms. Brown couldn't hold it any longer. She ran to his crumpled frame and began pounding him. "You the devil! Nothin' but the devil! You evil bastard! Damn you, damn you to hell!"

Det. Scott thrashed forward and knocked Ms. Brown down as he stood, gun in hand.

"You old bitch, I'm in hell! You hear me, I'm in hell! The woman I loved is dead!"

"Because you killed her." The sound of the male voice came from the door.

Det. Scott looked up to see Nilo standing in the door, his gun aimed at Scott.

"You killed her, you sick son of a bitch! How could you?"

Det. Scott smirked. "It's a dirty job..."

"So now, you come to confess and then kill the grandmother? Not today, pal! Drop the gun!"

"This?" Det. Scott asked, referring to the gun. "It isn't for her, it's for me."

With that, he raised the gun to his temple and blew his brain all over the wall. Ms. Brown folded in Det. Nilo's arms. It was finally over. Det. Nilo looked at the dead body of Det. Scott and thought how sick the world really was. Det. Scott had acted strange throughout the whole investigation and Det. Nilo's cop sixth sense wouldn't let it rest. After Det. Nilo had left the precinct, he went to Det. Scott's apartment. He didn't have to look far. All over his bedroom wall were pictures of Delilah, either alone or with Big Rock. But everywhere Big Rock was, Det. Scott had cut his face out of the picture and replaced it with his own. Det. Nilo knew then and rushed to Ms. Brown's home.

It truly was finally over.

The streets had claimed another in it's on going blood bath. These people were sickos and criminals. Det. Nilo vowed to clean up this mess once he became borough president. Det. Scott's dead body was just the stepping-stone he needed to get there.

The End.

TRIPLE CROWN PUBLICATIONS

ORDER FORM
Triple Crown Publications
2959 Stelzer Rd.
Columbus, OH 43219

NAME	
ADDRESS	
CITY	
STATE	
ZIP	

BOOKS AVAILABLE

#	TITLE	PRICE
	Gangsta	$15.00
	Let That Be The Reason	$15.00
	A Hustler's Wife	$15.00
	The Game	$15.00
	Black	$15.00
	Dollar Bill	$15.00
	A Project Chick	$15.00
	Road Dawgz	$15.00
	Blinded	$15.00
	Diva	$15.00
	Sheisty	$15.00
	Grimey	$15.00
	Me & My Boyfriend	$15.00
	Larceny	$15.00
	Rage Times Fury	$15.00
	A Hood Legend	$15.00
	Flipside of The Game	$15.00

SHIPPING/HANDLING (Via U.S.   **$ 3.50**
Priority Mail)

TOTAL   **$_____**

FORMS OF ACCEPTED PAYMENTS:
**Postage Stamps, Institutional Checks & Money
Orders, all mail in orders take 5-7 Business
Business days to be delivered**